Posters on the walls

Robert Rigby

LONDON • PRINCETON

www.two-canpublishing.com

Published by Two-Can Publishing,
43-45 Dorset Street, London W1H 4AB

For information on Two-Can books and multimedia,
call (0)20 7224 2440, fax (0)20 7224 7005, or visit
our website at http://www.two-canpublishing.com

Designed and edited by
Picthall & Gunzi Ltd,
21A Widmore Road,
Bromley BR1 1RW

Text by Robert Rigby

The *Byker Books* series is based on the major BBC TV
series *Byker Grove*, produced by Zenith North

Two-Can Publishing is a division of Zenith Entertainment plc,
43-45 Dorset Street, London W1H 4AB.

ISBN 1–85434–892–2

10 9 8 7 6 5 4 3 2 1

A catalogue record for this book is available from the British Library.

Cover photographs: Andrew Smith as Ben, Nicola Hetherington as Alice,
Holly Wilkinson as Emma, Jade Turnbull as Regina and Siobhan Hanratty as Nikki

Printed by Clays Ltd., Bungay, Suffolk

About the author

Robert Rigby began his career as a journalist, then spent several years in the music business as a songwriter and session musician. Now living in Norfolk, he has become an established young people's playwright, and his award-winning work with youth theatre companies has been seen in Britain, Europe and Africa. His plays for children include *Norah's Ark*, *My Friend Willy*, *Almost Human* and *Dance to my Tune*. Robert also writes scripts and music for television and radio. He composed the theme and incidental music for the BBC Radio Four drama series, *Mutiny on the Bounty*, which won the 1997 Talkies Best Production Award.

Posters on the walls

Alice stared at her half-eaten burger. She didn't want it. Outside it was still raining heavily, and great streaks of water were running down the huge, plate glass windows of the burger bar. They look like tears, thought Alice. She felt as miserable as the day.

"What's the matter, love?" asked her dad, cramming the last of his fries into his mouth. "I thought you liked burgers."

Alice sighed. "I do like them, Dad," she said, "but not every Sunday."

"Should have had something different," replied her dad, "there's plenty to choose from. Chicken nuggets? You should have had chicken nuggets."

Alice shook her head. Her dad didn't understand. The burger bar was almost empty; no-one wanted to go out on a day like this. Alice's eyes rested on a girl sitting on the far side of the room. She was about her age and was with a younger boy and a man. Alice knew the man was their dad. The girl looked up and saw Alice watching her, and as their eyes met, she smiled and gave a slight shrug of her shoulders. It's like a club, thought Alice, a club for dads and kids with nowhere to go.

Alice's dad drained the last few drops of tea from his beaker. "We don't come here every week," he said. "We went to your gran's last Sunday."

"Yeah," said Alice, remembering the visit to her grandparents the previous week. They were nice. She loved them. But they were old. They didn't really do anything. Most of the time they just sat and asked her questions, or watched television programmes that she didn't want to see, programmes about old people singing hymns or old people with antiques.

"It'll be easier soon, Alice," said her dad, reaching across the table and taking one of her hands in his. "When me and Cheryl have got a proper place, you'll have a room of your own. I'll decorate it however you like, you can keep some of your things there, put posters on the walls. It'll be your home."

"My home's with Mum," snapped Alice, snatching her hand away. "It'll always be with Mum."

The girl on the far side of the room was leaving. As she and her dad and brother walked towards the doors she glanced back at Alice, smiled, and waved.

"D'you know her?" asked Alice's dad.

"No," replied Alice, returning the wave. She turned to her father. "Are you and Cheryl going to get married?"

"Give us a chance, love," he answered, laughing nervously. "I'm not even divorced yet."

"But when you are? Will you then?"

"I'm not sure, we haven't decided. Maybe."

"Maybe you won't get divorced. Maybe you and Mum might..."

"Alice!"

Alice turned away as her dad continued. "You know your mum and me won't be getting back together. We've told you."

They were silent for a moment. Alice's dad picked up his beaker, remembered that it was empty and put it down again. "Would you like it if me and Cheryl got married?"

"I don't want you to get divorced," said Alice softly. "I don't know why this had to happen."

"I've explained," said her dad. "No-one wanted it to happen. It just did. We have to make the best of it. You do like Cheryl, don't you?"

"You're always asking me that," said Alice.

"She likes you."

"And you're always telling me that."

"Look, Alice," said her dad, "it'll all sort itself out. Just give it time."

Give it time. He always says that as well, thought Alice, especially when he wants to change the subject.

"Anyway, we should be talking about the next couple of weeks," said her dad. "Are you looking forward to going to Emma's?"

Alice shrugged. "S'pose so," she replied. "I quite liked her when we saw them last time."

"It'll be great," said her dad. "I used to love staying with my cousins when I was a kid."

Alice gazed out of the window. "Can we go now?" she asked. "It's stopped raining."

• • • • •

The general room at Byker Grove was virtually deserted. It was early in the session, and many of the Grovers had not yet arrived, but in one corner of the room Regina and her gang were huddled around a table. "And we're all responsible," Regina told the others sternly. "It's up to everyone, all of us – we can't just leave it to someone else." She paused and looked at her friends one by one. "So what are you gonna do, then?"

No-one answered. Laura looked at Barry, Barry looked at Bradley, Bradley looked at Stumpy, Stumpy looked at his dog Wombat, and Wombat looked away.

"Well?" demanded Regina. "You must have some suggestions. It's the future of the whole world we're talking about."

Still no-one answered. "Oh, you lot are useless," said Regina. "I'll have to show you, as usual."

She pushed away her chair and marched over to the light switch. "We can make a start in here," she said, clicking off one of the lights. "That's better. Follow me."

No-one moved. "Come on," urged Regina. "There's not much time." Reluctantly, Regina's friends hauled themselves up from their chairs and trailed behind her as she strode out into the corridor. Regina stopped. Her friends stopped. Regina looked up. The ceiling lights were shining brightly. Regina sighed and turned to her friends. "See what I mean?" she said, pointing dramatically up at the lights. "It's disgusting." She reached for the switch and another light went out. "That's quite bright enough," said Regina. "This way." She stomped on. The others followed. Obediently.

In the pool room, Ben was deep in concentration as he prepared for his shot. His eyes were fixed on the white ball. It was a long shot, black into the top left-hand pocket, not easy, but if he made it the game was his. Ollie looked on. He usually had the edge when he played Ben at pool, but this time defeat seemed inevitable.

Ben's mouth was dry. He swallowed nervously and breathed deeply. "Relax," he told himself, as he lined up the shot. "Just relax and keep your eyes on the ball. Nice and firm with plenty of backspin." He really wanted this game. Ollie was always boasting that he was easy to beat. Ben's cue arm moved smoothly backwards and forwards as he rehearsed the shot one final time. He was ready. "Now," he whispered, pushing the cue firmly forwards.

Then the lights went out.

There was a hollow, scratching sound as Ben's cue grazed the side of the white ball and sent it skidding away in completely the wrong direction. It missed the black, bounced off one of the side cushions, rebounded off the top cushion, and then crashed into the other side cushion before beginning its journey back down the table. Ben's eyes followed the ball as it glided past his left shoulder and rolled on towards the bottom left pocket. It was slowing down. Slower and slower it rolled as closer and closer it got to the pocket. It had almost stopped and, for a moment, it seemed as though it would come to a halt balanced on the very edge. But as Ben stared, willing the ball to stay up, it gave one final roll and toppled into the pocket.

"Oh, dear," said Ollie with a grin. "Unlucky, mate. Maybe you needed a bit more chalk. That's two shots to me, then."

Ben was still crouched over the table. Slowly he turned his head and saw Regina framed in the doorway. Her hand hovered over the light switch. "You," said Ben. "I might have known it. You!"

Regina smiled. "Whoops," she said. "Sorry. I didn't see you there."

"Didn't see me! Sorry!" said Ben furiously. He stood up. "What's the good in being sorry? You made me miss the shot!"

"Well, I'm sorry," said Regina. "But this is important."

"Important! What's important?"

A head appeared around the doorway. It was Bradley. "She's saving the world," he said, from the safety of the corridor.

"What?" shouted Ben.

Bradley's head disappeared.

Ben turned back to Regina. "What's he talking about?"

"I'm saving energy," said Regina enthusiastically. "We've all got to do something. They told us at school. If we want the world to survive it's up to all of us to do something. Switch off lights, turn down heating, and use less water. We've got to stop wasting energy."

Ben's grip tightened on the pool cue. "If you lot don't clear off," he said, "I'll waste some of my energy on you." He took one step towards Regina. Before he could take a second there was a flurry of activity in the doorway and the corridor and the young Grovers were gone.

Ben sighed and turned back to the pool table. Ollie had already removed the white ball from the pocket and was lining up his own, far easier, shot to the black. "Dunno about saving the world," he said. He took the shot. The white ball hit the black and sent it smoothly into the top pocket. "But she certainly saved me the game." He stood up and smiled at Ben. "Fancy trying again?"

"Typical," said Regina, as she and the others went back into the general room. "More interested in a game of pool than the future of the planet. And it's not my fault if he's a useless player." She stopped. "Who turned all the lights back on in here?"

"I did," answered Emma, who had just arrived. "It was dark. Gloomy. And I don't want to feel gloomy. My cousin's coming to stay."

"We've got more important things to worry about than cousins," said Regina.

Her friends had decided otherwise. "Boy or girl?" asked Barry. "We could do with more boys around here."

"Speak for yourself," said Regina. "Now, about our campaign to save…"

"*Your* campaign," said Laura, butting in. "Can't we give it a rest for a while?"

"Yeah," added Barry and Bradley in unison.

"Yeah," echoed Stumpy. "Wombat wants to know about Emma's cousin. Don't you, Wombat?"

Stumpy's faithful dog didn't appear to want to know about anything. He gave an enormous yawn, lifted a back paw and scratched frantically behind one ear, collapsed on to the floor and closed his eyes.

Emma smiled. "She's a girl. Her name's Alice."

"What's she like?" asked Laura.

"She's really nice. A bit quiet."
"Like me then," said Regina.
"No, Regina," said Emma, "she's nothing like you. Except..."
"Yeah? Except what?"
"Well, I suppose she is like you in one way."
"What way?"
"Her mum and dad have split up."
"Oh," said Regina dismissively. "Well, there's nothing unusual in that, is there?"

• • • • •

Emma sat on her bed. She was watching her cousin unpack her suitcase. "It's all arranged," she said, trying to sound as cheerful as possible. "You're an official temporary member of Byker Grove."
"Oh," said Alice. She didn't sound enthusiastic. "Good."
Emma tried again. "It's great at the Grove. Loads to do. You can do whatever you like. And I've got hundreds of mates." Emma stopped and reconsidered, realising she was sounding a little too enthusiastic. "Well, quite a few. I've told them all about you."
Alice snapped her suitcase shut and turned to her cousin. "All about me! What d'you mean, all about me? What have you said?"
Emma stared, taken aback by the sudden anger in her cousin's voice. "Just... just about you. That you're my cousin and that you're staying and... and..."
"And that my mum and dad have split up and my dad's got himself a new girlfriend?"
"No!" answered Emma. "Well... yes, I suppose I did, but not about your dad's new..."
"What if I didn't want them to know? What if I didn't want anyone to know? It's none of their business. Or yours. It's nobody's business but mine." Alice slumped unhappily down on to the campbed that had been put up for her stay. She looked down at the floor. "You shouldn't have said anything," she whispered. "You shouldn't have said anything."
"I'm sorry," said Emma quietly. "I didn't realise."
Emma had been looking forward to her cousin's stay. Alice was

nearly a year older than Emma, and Emma wanted to show her off at the Grove and introduce her to her friends, specially the older ones. But so far it wasn't going quite the way Emma had imagined. She had never known her cousin to be like this. They didn't see each other very often, but when they did they always got on well. Until now. Alice had been sullen and moody all afternoon, and when her dad had left after dropping her off, she hardly bothered to say goodbye.

"They won't be talking about you, Alice," said Emma. "They don't care. A lot of them are like you."

"Like me?" asked her cousin.

"I mean, they're in the same sort of situation as you. Their parents have split up. Some of them live in a foster home. My friend Regina lives with her uncle. At least you still live with your mum and you do see your dad."

"Oh, and that's supposed to be good, is it?" asked Alice, not really expecting an answer.

She didn't get one. Emma didn't know what to say.

Alice gazed around her cousin's bedroom. It was much like her own. Untidy. There were clothes draped over the back of a chair. There was a clutter of paper, coloured bottles, pieces of jewellery and framed photographs on the white dressing table. And there were posters on the walls. Alice's eyes rested on the posters. "I like your posters," she said. "My dad says that when they get a proper place I'll have my own bedroom and I can put posters up, just like at home."

Emma still wasn't sure what she was supposed to say. "That'll be good. Won't it?"

"No, it won't be good," said Alice. "How can it be good? It won't be my home and she's not my mum. I hardly know her. How can it ever be good?"

"I… I…" Emma had no answer to Alice's question. "What's she like?" she asked. "Your dad's… you know…"

"Cheryl," said Alice. "Her name's Cheryl. She's alright. She's nice enough to me. She never says much when I'm with them. She never tells me off, or blames me if something goes wrong, or shouts at me like my mum does. But I wish she would."

"What?" asked a bewildered Emma.

"Just sometimes," said Alice. "Then it'd be more… normal. More real. It's like it's not real when I'm with them. And my dad's different. He's like a different person since he's been with her."

Emma got off her own bed and went and sat next to her cousin. "You'll get used to it in time," she said, putting one arm around Alice's shoulders.

"I've heard that before," replied Alice.

There was a knock on the bedroom door. "Can I come in, girls?" called Emma's mum as she opened the door and walked into the room.

"You are in," replied Emma, taking her arm from Alice's shoulders.

Emma's mum smiled at Alice. "Settling in alright, pet?"

"Fine thanks, Auntie Jackie," replied Alice.

"All unpacked?"

Alice nodded.

"Emma's made some space for your clothes in her wardrobe. Have you shown her, Emma?"

"Yes, Mum," said Emma.

"And I'm sure you're much tidier with your things than she is." She turned to her daughter. "I thought I told you to tidy up this room."

"I have tidied it," replied Emma indignantly. "It is tidy. Took me ages to do this."

Her mother laughed. "See what I mean, Alice? Now, get yourselves ready, we're going out."

"Out? Oh, Mum," moaned Emma. "I wanted to take Alice to the Grove."

"There's plenty of time for the Grove," said her mum. "You've got two weeks to go to the Grove. Sometimes I think you live at that place and just stop off here for your meals."

"But..."

"And no 'buts'. It's Alice's first night here and we're going out. Special treat. Your dad's taking us all to the burger bar. You love burgers don't you, Alice? I remember from last time."

Alice sighed. Being nice to me, she thought. She's being nice to me. Why does everyone think they've got to be nice to me? She smiled at her aunt. "Yes, Auntie Jackie," she said, "I love burgers."

• • • • •

"Well, I don't think she's very nice. I think she's a right misery." Regina was not impressed by Alice. "I told her about my saving energy campaign. I told her everyone was getting involved. She just ignored me."

Regina and Laura were on their way in to the Grove. Liam was on his way out. "Most people seem to ignore you, Regina," he said with a smile as he brushed past the two girls at the doorway.

"It's rude to listen to other people's conversations," Regina shouted after him. "And where are you going? Everyone's supposed to be here."

"I haven't got time for kids' games," yelled Liam, without looking back.

"It's not a game. It's serious," shouted Regina. She turned to Laura. "He'll be sorry."

"Regina, we're late," said Laura.

"I know, but just listen before we go in. I was in the toilets yesterday and Alice came in with Emma, and I heard her say she didn't think much of the Grove. What a cheek!"

"You just told Liam it's rude to listen to other people's conversations," said Laura.

"I wasn't listening, I just happened to overhear them. I couldn't help it, could I? Come on."

The two girls hurried along the corridor into the general room. It was crowded; almost everyone was there, both young and older Grovers. "About time," said Teraise. "You're late."

"Sorry. We got held up," said Regina.

"Dunno what we're all sitting around here for anyway," said Nat. "Haven't we heard enough about Regina and energy. It's tiring me out."

The older Grovers didn't appreciate being kept waiting by a twelve-year-old. "You asked us to be here, Regina," said Ollie. "And we've already agreed to your plan. What now?"

"Give her a chance," said Sita. "We've waited this long."

Regina stepped on to the stage. She wanted to be sure that everyone could see her. "I apologise for being late," she said, "but the reason I called this meeting is because I knew you'd all want to hear about my press conference."

"Your what?" asked Nat.

"Oh, here we go," said Ben.

"Press what?" asked Stumpy.

"Little Regina's dreaming again," said Cher.

"I'm not dreaming, it's true," said Regina.

"Yeah, right," said Cher.

"Tell them Laura," said Regina. "You were there."

Laura nodded. "It wasn't exactly a press conference, but we did go to the *Byker Post*.

"And they interviewed me," said Regina.

"Us," said Laura.

"And they took my photo," said Regina.

"Our photo," corrected Laura.

"And they told us there'll be a picture and a story in tomorrow's paper," said Regina.

Ben wasn't convinced. "What do they want to put your ugly mugs in the paper for?"

"Because they think my saving energy plan is great. They said so. I told them we were having a special day here and I told them about our poster competition, and they said it's a brilliant way to get the message over. They said I was..." Regina paused and glanced at Laura. "They said we were a credit to the Grove. Didn't they, Laura?"

Laura nodded. The general room was silent. Regina could see the Grovers were impressed but she wasn't quite finished. "And," she added, saving the best for last, "the man at the *Byker Post* said they'd print thousands of copies of the winning poster."

"What for?" asked Stumpy.

"Oh, Stumpy," said Laura, embarrassed as usual by her younger brother.

"So they can be put up in shops and offices and schools," said Regina. "I told you it was important. I told you we all had to do something. Well, now we are. Our poster will be all over the town, maybe all over the city."

"Who's gonna pick the winner, then?" asked Bradley. "You can't be the judge, Regina. You're doing a poster yourself."

Karen stepped forward and joined Regina on the stage. "She's not the judge," she said. "We're the judges. Me and Cher and Sita."

"You said you didn't want to do it," said Regina, looking up at Karen.

Karen smiled. "Oh, yeah, but that was before."

"Before what?"

"Before it was gonna be in the paper. They'll probably want a picture of the judges with the winning poster. They'll need a bit of glamour."

"Won't want you lot then," said Nat.

Karen ignored her. "So you'd all better get on with your designs. We're gonna be picking the winner on…" She turned to Regina. "When is it?"

"Friday."

"Oh, yeah. We're gonna be picking the winner on Friday."

"But why should you three be the judges?" asked Bradley.

"Because we're experienced designers ourselves," said Cher.

Nat laughed. "What, those clothes you did last year?"

Cher nodded. "Yeah," she said. "Everyone said our designs were fantastic."

"Did they?" said Nat. "I thought they were rubbish."

Cher smiled sweetly at Nat. "Jealous as usual, are we?"

"Jealous of you lot?" replied Nat with a sneer. "That'll be the day."

Regina allowed herself a smile of satisfaction. She had worked hard to persuade everyone at the Grove that it was vital for them all to take part in her energy-saving campaign. It hadn't been easy, it had taken several days, but Regina was determined, and she had a plan.

First she pestered her own gang of friends until they couldn't be bothered to argue anymore. Then she targeted Nikki and her boyfriend, Matt, who already believed in doing anything they could to help the environment. That was the easy bit. With Nikki and Matt on her side, Regina was able to recruit several of the older Grovers. But there were still some doubters, so Regina made her finest move by announcing to everyone at the Grove: "We'll be holding the Byker Grove *Don't Waste Energy Day*. And it'll be brilliant fun."

"Fun? How's that supposed to be fun?" Ollie had asked.

"Because for one whole day we use less energy. We turn down the heating, we turn off some of the lights, and the DJ decks, and the television and the drinks machines. We don't waste hot water, all that sort of thing."

"Oh, yeah, terrific. That sounds like great fun. I don't think."

But Regina wasn't finished: "Yes, but after the *Don't Waste Energy Day* we have the *Don't Waste Energy Night*. A party. That's where the fun comes in. And we can do it. I've already got permission."

And she had. Tina, the Grove's youth worker, had agreed to supervise Regina's open-air, candlelit, energy-saving party. "We'll have a bonfire and a barbecue," she told the Grovers. "And we can make our own entertainment, like they did in the old days. No DJ decks or electric music, though. We won't use any electricity. It'll be Byker Grove – unplugged."

"Byker Grove – unplugged," Ben said. "It's good. I like it."

Everyone liked it, even though some of the older members of Byker Grove didn't want to appear too enthusiastic about an idea dreamt up by one of the youngest Grovers.

"Be a laugh," Ollie said to Ben. "You can get up to all sorts in the dark."

And so the preparations for the Byker Grove *Don't Waste Energy Day* and the poster competition, which had been suggested by Laura, mainly as a way of stopping Regina from going on and on at them, had been put into action.

Now Regina had scored another triumph with her news of the article and photograph in the *Byker Post*. The meeting broke up and there was much discussion as the Grovers drifted away to various rooms and distant corners of the building.

"I might have a go at this poster competition after all," Nat said to Claire as they walked into the corridor. "I'm good at Art."

"I didn't know that," replied Claire.

"Well, better than Cher and her lot, anyway. Let's get some paper from the office."

Barry, Bradley, Stumpy and Wombat made their way towards the front door. "I told my mum about all this saving energy stuff," said Stumpy. "I said the best thing I could do was to save water and gas by only having a bath once a month."

"What did she say?" asked Barry.

"What d'you think?" replied Stumpy. "Still, it was worth a try." He stepped through the open doorway. "Come on," he said. "Wombat wants a run around."

Emma and her cousin Alice had remained in the general room, which by now was almost empty. It was the fourth day of Alice's visit and she had become a familiar, if not particularly popular, figure at the Grove.

Emma's friends had tried to make her welcome. On Alice's very first day Bradley and Barry took her on a guided tour of the building, and Nikki, seeing Alice on her own, began a conversation. But it proved to be a one-way conversation with Nikki doing all the talking, and she soon gave up.

Then Ben attempted to impress Alice by showing her how to make the drinks machine work by kicking it in the right place. Alice wasn't impressed.

"I think Ben likes you," Emma had said that evening. Alice had simply shrugged. She didn't seem to be interested in anyone or anything.

Emma sighed. Spending a holiday with her cousin was proving to be no fun at all. "Are you going to do a poster for the competition?" she asked.

"No," said Alice. "I think it's stupid."

"Well, I don't. I'm doing one."

"Who's that boy over there? In the wheelchair. I haven't seen him here before."

Greg had been sitting on the far side of the room throughout the meeting. Now he was gazing out through the conservatory windows. The muffled sounds of shouting and laughter and Wombat's barking could just be heard as Greg watched some of the younger boys scramble over the climbing frame.

"It's Greg," said Emma. "He's Nikki's brother."

"Has he always been like that?"

"Like what?"

"In a wheelchair."

"No, he hasn't," said Emma. "Not for very long. He... he had an accident."

"He looks miserable."

The past four days had been difficult for Emma. She had put up with Alice's silences, her sudden outbursts of temper and her tears. She had put up with a lot. But she had put up with enough.

"Well, wouldn't you look miserable?" she snapped. "Wouldn't you look miserable if you'd been told you might have to spend the rest of your life in a wheelchair? Wouldn't you look miserable if you couldn't just stand up and walk out?" She stood up and pushed her chair away. The metal chair legs scraped and grated across the floor. "Like I'm going to do now!"

Emma rushed from the room and Alice felt her cheeks redden.

She glanced over to where Greg was sitting. He had heard the noise of the chair and was staring at her. Alice looked away. There were tears in her eyes.

• • • • •

"It's not worth getting in a state over," said Nikki. "Here, take some of these." She passed Emma a handful of tissues and Emma wiped her eyes. She blew her nose loudly.

Emma had run straight from the activities room to the girls' toilets. She hadn't wanted to cry but she couldn't stop herself. Nikki had come in a few minutes later.

"I don't know what to do, Nikki," said Emma. "I know she's unhappy about her parents but it's not my fault. She's ruining the holiday. I just want her to go home."

"She probably needs to talk to someone about it," said Nikki. "I know I did."

"Did you? Well, do you think you could talk to her?" asked Emma.

"Me?" said Nikki. "I'm not exactly an expert when it comes to parents and step-parents."

"But at least you've been through something like this. I just don't know what to say. Every night when we go to bed she goes on and on, about her dad, and her mum, and her dad's new girlfriend. Could you, Nikki? Please?"

"I don't know," said Nikki. "I'm still trying to forget the trouble I had with my step-father. But maybe. I'll think about it, Emma."

"Thanks," said Emma. She wiped her eyes again. "I suppose I'd better go and find her and tell her I'm sorry. Trouble is, I'm not. Not really."

"Are you sure you're alright?"

"Yeah, I'm fine."

The two girls went back to the general room. Alice had gone. Greg was alone, still gazing out through the window.

"D'you know where Alice went, Greg?" asked Emma.

"Who's Alice?" said Greg, without looking back at Emma and his sister.

"She was with me," said Alice. "My cousin."

Greg shook his head. "How should I know? She went out."
"Oh, no," said Emma to Nikki. "I'd better go and find her."
"D'you want me to come with you?"
"No, I'll do it. You stay here with Greg."
"You don't have to stay with me," said Greg. "I'm alright."
Nikki looked at Emma. "See you later," she said.
"Yeah," said Emma. "See you later." She walked towards the door, but then stopped and turned back. She had liked Greg since long before his accident. "Bye, Greg," she called.
There was no reply.
Emma searched the entire Grove but she didn't find her cousin. She looked in the office, then in the games room, and then in the pool room. She went down to the cellar and up to the attic, but as she climbed the stairs Emma felt certain that Alice was no longer at the Grove. No-one had seen her since the meeting, but then, no-one had particularly wanted to see her.
Emma came back down the stairs and decided that she ought to look outside. She knew she was wasting her time, but she went out through the front door and walked round to the back of the Grove. It was quiet now the boys had gone. Emma searched in the car park, through the adventure playground, by the pond and in the trees at the very back of the grounds. But Alice wasn't there. Alice had gone.
"She must have gone home," Emma said out loud, as she came back to the front door and stood with her back to the driveway. "Now Mum'll have a go at me for not staying with her."
Emma heard footsteps approaching and she turned, expecting for a moment to see her cousin. But it wasn't Alice.
"Talking to yourself, eh? That's not a good sign," said Ben. "Why are you hanging around out here?"
"I'm looking for my cousin. Have you seen her?"
"Not since the meeting. What's wrong with her? I don't think I've seen her smile once since she got here. Pity, she's quite nice-looking."
"It's her parents. They split up and her dad's got a new girlfriend."
Ben shook his head and smiled.
"Why are you smiling?" asked Emma.
"Parents," said Ben. "I don't know why we bother with them. They're more trouble than they're worth."
"Mine are alright," said Emma.

"Yeah, well you're lucky then. So far. My dad's in prison and I don't remember my mum. Tell your cousin to come and talk to me if she wants to know about parents."

Ben turned to go into the Grove, but Emma called after him. "Ben?"

"Yeah?" said Ben, stopping in the doorway.

"Do you mean that? Could she really talk to you?"

Ben hesitated. "Well… yeah… I suppose so. If you think it will do any good."

• • • • •

Alice was at home when Emma returned but, fortunately for Emma, her mum wasn't. That evening the two girls hardly spoke, and it didn't get better over the next couple of days. Emma and Alice grew further and further apart. They walked to the Grove together, they walked home together, but while Emma chatted to her friends or worked on her poster, Alice sat alone or drifted aimlessly around the building or the grounds.

The Grove was busy and bustling. Many of the Grovers were designing posters and writing energy-saving slogans. Regina marched around with a list of things to do for *Don't Waste Energy Day* and the party. She announced that all the finished posters were to be displayed on the general room walls by last thing Thursday evening in readiness for the judging on Friday.

"And," she told the Grovers, "no names on the front of the posters. Write them on the back." She gave a warning look at Sita, Cher and Karen. "I don't want any favouritism from the judges. It has to be completely fair."

Sita, Karen and Cher just laughed and went back to their rehearsal. They were preparing some new songs for the party. In another room Bradley divided his time between painting a poster and perfecting his magic tricks.

Ben hadn't forgotten his offer to speak to Alice. In fact, he wanted to speak to her. He had smiled at her, nodded to her, winked at her, but so far, since his first attempt at the drinks machine, he hadn't actually managed to talk to her again.

"What d'you keep smiling at that girl for?" Ollie asked, when he caught Ben glancing in Alice's direction.

"Just being friendly," said Ben. "What's wrong with that?"

"Yeah?" replied Ollie with a grin. "You fancy her, don't you?"

"She's alright," answered Ben.

"Go and use your famous charm on her, then," said Ollie. "Might work for a change."

"Yeah, maybe," said Ben. "Later."

Gradually the finished posters began to appear on the walls of the general room and by mid-afternoon on Thursday they were almost all in place.

"Look great, don't they?" said Tina to Regina. "I didn't know we had so many talented artists at the Grove."

"It's alright for them," Regina replied. "I hardly had time to work on mine. There's so much to do. I've got to go and decide on the best sites for the bonfire and the barbecue now."

Tina smiled. "Well, when you decide, make sure you check with me," she said.

Regina hurried away, clutching a clipboard in one hand and a well-worn pencil in the other. She went out into the grounds of Byker Grove. It was a blustery day. Regina pulled up the collar on her coat and walked quickly round to the side of the building.

"Can't have a bonfire too near the car park," she told herself. "Or near the playground or the pond. Someone's bound to fall in."

She wandered on, searching for an area large enough and open enough for the party. "I know," she said. "Further round to the back. That's the place." She walked on. It really was windy. "I hope it's not like this for the party," Regina told herself.

She reached the back of the building and stopped. Someone was sitting on one of the wooden benches. Whoever it was wore a fleece jacket with the collar pulled straight up. All Regina could see was the top of a head. She frowned and walked on and the figure on the bench slowly turned as Regina approached. It was Alice.

"What are you sitting out here for?" asked Regina. "It's freezing."

"I know you think you own the place," said Alice coldly, "but I don't have to ask your permission for where I sit, do I?"

Regina was not famous at the Grove for her sympathy and understanding. She had been through difficult times, never really knowing her father and spending years living apart from her mother.

Now, even though she had rebuilt a relationship with her mother, she still lived with her uncle and her cousin, Teraise. But Regina wasn't the sort of person to let personal problems dominate the whole of her life.

"I know you're unhappy about your mum and dad," she said, "but it's no good being miserable all the time."

"I don't need your advice, thanks," said Alice.

"If you're not happy, you have to do something about it. I did."

"You? What did you do?"

"My mum… Well, she wasn't… she wasn't interested in me. Just in herself. She can't help it, that's the way she is. So I divorced her."

Alice stared at Regina. "Divorced her? What do you mean?"

"I decided that if she wasn't interested in me, then I wouldn't be interested in her. So I left her. I came to live with my uncle. Mum didn't seem to mind too much at the time."

Alice sat up. She had been deep in her own thoughts before Regina arrived. Since her parents separated three months ago it seemed to Alice as though her whole world had been shaken apart. She hadn't even known that her parents were unhappy. Sometimes they argued, or shouted, or sulked with each other, but Alice just thought that all parents were like that.

Then one day Alice arrived home from school to find her mum in tears and her dad waiting to say goodbye. There were two suitcases standing by the front door. Nothing would change, her dad told her, they both still loved her, it was just that they couldn't live together anymore.

Alice had cried and begged her dad not to leave them. But he did, without telling Alice that he was going to live with someone else. Her mum had been left to do that, and a few weeks later, even though she didn't want to do it, Alice had agreed to meet Cheryl for the first time. It was awkward. Uncomfortable. How could she possibly like her? How could they ever be friends? She was the person who had taken her dad away.

Alice turned to Regina. "And did you feel better? For doing it?"

Regina shrugged. "At least I knew where I was, even if I didn't know where my mum was."

It was getting colder and Regina found herself beginning to shiver. She had been sympathetic and she had listened, but now her patience was growing thin.

"Why don't you just come inside and do a poster?" she said, a little too sharply.

"I don't want to do a poster," said Alice. "I think the whole thing's stupid."

Regina snapped. "Look, you've been hanging around here all week, looking miserable, feeling sorry for yourself. It's not fair on Emma; it's not fair on any of us. Why don't you just grow up and pull yourself together?"

Alice stood up angrily. Her eyes were blazing. "Just leave me alone, will you? Stupid kid!"

She stormed away leaving Regina staring after her. "That's what you get for trying to help," she said to herself.

Alice ran back into the Grove. She didn't want to see her cousin or her friends, she didn't really want to see anyone, but she was cold and she needed to be inside. She went into the pool room.

Ben was alone at the table, practising. He looked up and saw Alice. Here was his chance. "Hello," he said with a smile. "Want a game?"

"I can't play snooker," said Alice.

Ben laughed. "It's pool," he said. "I'll teach you."

"Well... oh, alright."

"Great," said Ben.

Ben found the wooden triangle and began to reset the pool balls. Several times during the week Alice had noticed Ben looking at her, but she had been too unhappy to think of anything but her own situation. Ben handed Alice a cue and leaned over the table to take a shot.

"You just rest the cue between your thumb and finger, like this," he said. "It's easy." He took the shot and the white ball crashed into the colours and scattered them around the table. "Your turn. You can go for anything you like, except the black."

Alice went to the table and awkwardly placed the cue between her thumb and finger as Ben had shown her. There were so many balls to aim for she could hardly miss. And she didn't.

"Good shot," said Ben.

"At least I hit one," said Alice with a smile.

Ben went back to the table, ready now to impress Alice with his skills. He lined up a shot and decided that now was also the moment to demonstrate to Alice how caring and considerate he could be.

"Emma told me about your parents," he said. "We can talk about it, if you want."

It was the wrong moment. Alice slammed the pool cue down on to the table. "You as well," she shouted. "Why don't you just leave me alone – all of you? Why can't you just mind your own business?" She walked out.

Ben stood up from the table and stared at the empty doorway. "Oh great," he said. "Nice one, Ben."

• • • • •

Regina had decided on the best places for the barbecue and the bonfire and was giving everyone at the Grove a guided tour of the party site. She pointed. "The food will be served there and we need to set up benches and tables over there." She looked at her clipboard. "Now, if you'll follow me, I'll show you where we'll be having the entertainment." Regina was in charge.

Alice was alone in the general room, everyone else was outside. She glared at the posters covering the walls. "Stupid," she said. "Stupid posters and stupid people. Trying to interfere – telling me what to do."

Alice felt confused and terribly unhappy. The posters were colourful and cheerful, and as Alice looked at them, they made her feel even more miserable. On one poster there was a huge, smiling, happy face, painted in bright yellow. It's horrible, thought Alice. Like it's laughing at me.

She walked over to the wall, reached for the poster and pulled. It came away easily.

"I'll stop them laughing," said Alice. "I'll stop them all laughing."

She reached for another poster and pulled it down from the wall. She reached for another, and then another. In seconds, nearly half the posters had been pulled from the walls. Alice wanted to rip them apart, tear them to pieces. But she couldn't do it. "I'll hide them," she whispered. "Put them where they won't find them. Stupid posters."

She went to the doorway and peered into the corridor. It was deserted. Byker Grove was silent. Upstairs, thought Alice. I'll hide them upstairs. Clutching the posters to her body, Alice crept into the corridor and, without looking back, she turned towards the stairs. Alice didn't see Ben as he walked in through the main doors. But Ben saw Alice. He went to call out, but stopped himself. He'd spotted the sheets of paper Alice held in her arms. So he followed. Quietly.

Ben had been worrying about Alice. He had trailed, with the others, through the grounds of Byker Grove as Regina told them of her plans for the party. But Ben wasn't listening. He was thinking about his encounter with Alice in the pool room. He'd got it wrong and he wanted to try again. As soon as a chance came to slip away, he took it.

He trod softly as he followed Alice. He glanced into the general room as he passed the open door and immediately saw the empty spaces on the walls where the posters had been.

"Oh, no," he whispered. "What's she playing at?" He walked on.

Alice reached the attic as Ben started to climb the stairs. She went in through the door. The dusty room was cluttered with boxes and old bits of electrical gear, and in one corner, leaning against the wall, was a broken DJ deck. It looked as though it hadn't been moved for months. "There," Alice whispered. "They'll never look there."

She hurried across the room and began sliding the posters into the small gap between the heavy DJ deck and the wall. It was difficult, the space was quite small, but Alice squeezed the posters in, one by one.

Alice was nervous. Frightened. She knew what she was doing was wrong. She knew she should stop and take the posters back before she was discovered. But it was too late for second thoughts. She had to go on.

A floorboard creaked and Alice froze. A footstep. Someone had followed her. Someone was watching her now. Alice stood up slowly. She turned around.

YOU DECIDE DOES BEN CONFRONT ALICE?

YES GO TO THE NEXT PAGE

NO GO TO PAGE 92

Ben was watching her from the open doorway.

"Ben," she gasped. "I... I..."

"Get them," said Ben. "Now. You've got to put them back before anyone sees what you've done."

Alice was trembling. She wanted to run away. She wanted to escape. But she couldn't move. She stood rooted to the spot, her eyes wide with terror.

"Hurry up," said Ben. "They'll be back inside any minute. Get the posters."

Alice still didn't move.

"Come on!" Ben urged.

Somehow Alice forced herself to go back to the DJ deck. She crouched down and reached into the gap. But retrieving the posters was more difficult than hiding them had been. The seconds passed. Slowly the posters began to reappear.

Alice pushed her arm deep into the gap. "There's one more," she said, straining to reach the last poster. "I can't reach..." Her fingers found the edge of the poster. She grabbed it and pulled, and she felt the paper tear.

"I've torn one! Ben, I've torn one!" cried Alice, as the poster emerged into the gloomy light of the attic.

"Never mind that now," said Ben. "Just get them downstairs and back on the walls. I'll go down and try to keep the others outside for as long as I can."

Ben turned and hurried to the stairs.

"Ben...?" called Alice. But it was too late. He was gone.

Alice gathered together the posters and ran to the stairs. Halfway down she stopped. She had to know whose poster she had torn. She saw the jagged tear, almost from one side to the other. Alice turned the poster over, and there, in bold, confident writing, was the name of the artist: Regina O'Hagan.

"Oh, no," moaned Alice. "Not hers!" Alice knew she had to go on. She reached the bottom of the stairs and rushed along the long corridor. But as she turned the corner leading to the general room she heard voices. The Grovers, led by Regina, were coming back into the building.

The voices stopped as Alice came to a halt. The Grovers were staring at her. For a minute no-one said a word. They just stared. At the back of the group was Ben. He shook his head sadly.

At last Emma broke the silence. "Alice... why... what have you done?"

"I'll tell you what she's done," said Regina savagely. "She's taken the posters. Look, she's torn them."

Alice tried to speak. "No... I didn't mean... it was an accident..."

Regina ran and snatched the torn poster from Alice's hands. "It's mine," she said, waving the poster at the other Grovers. "She had to spoil my poster first. She didn't have time to ruin the rest."

"No, it wasn't like that," said Alice. "I didn't know it was yours. It was an accident."

"Oh, sure it was. Just because you didn't like what I said..."

"Just a minute, Regina," said Tina. "There's no point in shouting. I'll sort this out."

Tina took the remaining posters from Alice's hands. "Do you want to tell us why you did this?" she asked quietly. "Do you want to explain?"

Alice did want to tell them. She did want to explain and beg their forgiveness. She looked at Tina, then at Regina, and then at the sea of hostile faces glaring at her.

"I... I..." she muttered. But she couldn't go on. She shook her head and took a step forwards. She was shaking, her legs felt so weak she almost fell. The Grovers stepped aside as she pushed her way through the group. She couldn't look at their faces, not even her cousin's. Only Ben watched Alice go as she reached the front door and went out.

Ben turned back to the other Grovers. "Look, maybe she didn't mean to do any harm. Maybe it was just a stupid..."

"Leave it, Ben," said Nat. "She ripped the poster. Regina's poster. It's obvious. She knew what she was doing."

Emma stared at the floor. She felt so ashamed. She knew, now that her cousin had gone, that most of the Grovers were looking at her.

Regina turned to Tina. "We don't want her back," she said coldly. "We want her banned from the Grove. She's hateful."

The other Grovers murmured in agreement.

• • • • •

Emma's mother sat at one side of the kitchen table and sipped her tea. Her daughter sat at the opposite side of the table, her head in her hands.

"She'll have to go home, Mum, she can't come back to the Grove. She's banned."

"Her dad'll be heart-broken. What in the world got into her?"

"She's been like it ever since she arrived. It's been horrible, and I was really looking forward to her being here."

"I'm sorry, pet, you shouldn't have to put up with this."

"I've tried, Mum, honestly."

"I know you have, pet." Emma's mum sighed. "Her dad's never been good at talking. It was the same when we were kids. Any problems and he'd just run away from them, or pretend they weren't happening and wait for someone else to sort them out. Well, it's about time he started facing up to things. He can't run away from this."

The front doorbell rang. "Oh, who's that now? You go, will you, Emma? I don't feel like seeing anyone."

Emma went to the front door and opened it. On the doorstep stood Ben. He looked nervous. "I asked Laura where you lived," he said. "There's something I've got to tell you."

"You'd better come in," said Emma. She led him through to the kitchen. "This is Ben, Mum," she said. "He goes to the Grove."

"Sit down, Ben," said Emma's mum with a smile. "What can we do for you?"

Ben didn't sit down. He stood by the sink, feeling as uncomfortable as he looked. "I'm not staying. I just wanted you to know that Alice wasn't going to destroy the posters, just hide them. I saw her. I followed her up to the attic and I saw her hide them."

"But why?" asked Emma's mum. "Why did she do it?"

Ben shrugged. "I told her she had to put them back and she was going to, but the others came in. Tearing Regina's poster was an accident. It was. Honest."

"Then why didn't she tell them that?"

"She was scared. Everyone could see that. I tried to tell them afterwards but they thought I was just trying to make excuses for her because…"

"Because?"

Ben didn't answer. He began to blush.

Emma's mum smiled. "Because you like Alice? Is that it Ben?"
Ben nodded.

"I'm glad," said Emma's mum. "Alice needs all the friends she can get at the moment."

"I know how she must be feeling," said Ben. "I mean, about her parents. My mum left us when I was a kid. I don't even remember her. And my dad, well... he's useless, and I... I wanted to help. I still do. She could always come round to Lou's."

"Lou?"

"Lou Gallagher. She runs the foster home where I live. Alice should talk to Lou. She's brilliant."

"I need another cup of tea," said Emma's mum. She went to the kettle and switched it on. "D'you want one, Ben?"

"No thanks," Ben replied. "I'd better be going. I'll leave the phone number of Gallagher's."

"Listen, Ben," said Emma's mum, as Ben wrote down the number. "We'll tell her you came. She's up in Emma's room at the moment. She's a bit tearful. But we'll tell her you came and what you said. And thanks. We really appreciate it."

Emma went up to her room after Ben had gone. She paused outside the door, wondering whether or not she should go in. She knocked on the door. There was no answer so Emma opened the door and went inside. Alice was lying on her bed, staring up at the ceiling.

"I know I shouldn't have done it," she said to Emma without looking at her. "And I'm sorry."

"Why didn't you tell them you were putting the posters back?"

Alice sat up. "How do you know that?"

"Ben was here. He told me and Mum. You should have told them, when you had the chance."

"They wouldn't have believed me. They all hate me."

Emma sat on her own bed. It had been a long day, she had been humiliated in front of her friends at the Grove and she was tired and fed up. "Oh, stop feeling sorry for yourself, Alice," she said. "Look, why don't you just go home?"

"I can't go home," snapped Alice. "I don't want to see my dad. This is all his fault, anyway. And my mum... I can't face her."

"Ben wants to talk to you," said Emma. "He left his phone number. He likes you."

"I don't know why," said Alice. She rolled over and buried her head in the pillow. "I can't talk to him. I don't want to talk to anyone. Not anyone."

The bedroom door swung open and Emma's mum came into the room. She was angry. "Right. That's enough of that talk. You're going to have to speak to someone, Alice. You can't carry on like this. And you can't treat Emma like this, either."

Alice jumped off the bed and went to her aunt. "Oh, please don't send me home, Auntie Jackie. I'm sorry for what I did, really I am. And I'll try to put it right. Tomorrow. I will. Really, I will."

Alice began to cry. Tears ran down her cheeks and she threw herself on the bed and sobbed. Emma looked at her mum. She was angry with her cousin, and hurt by what she had done. But she knew that Alice's hurt was far more than her own. She moved to Alice's bed and put an arm around her cousin.

"It's alright, Alice," she said. "We'll put it right. Tomorrow."

Emma's mum shook her head and sighed. "Tomorrow," she said.

• • • • •

Emma and Alice were in town. It was the following morning, Friday, the day the poster competition was to be judged. At breakfast, Alice had told Emma that she really did want to go to the Grove and apologise for all the trouble she had caused.

"But later," she had added. "Let's go into town for a while. Maybe we'll buy something."

The girls had finished their breakfast and walked into town and, gradually, Alice became more like the cousin Emma remembered.

She chatted as they looked in shop windows. She giggled as they tried on clothes that neither of them could afford. She laughed when a group of boys tried to chat them up. She didn't mention her dad or her mum or how unhappy she was feeling. She looked different. She was smiling.

They sat on a bench in the town centre. It was a bright day, warm and sunny. Alice delved into the plastic bag she was carrying and took out two sandwiches they had bought earlier. "Tuna and sweet corn for you, and BLT for me," she said.

"I don't like bacon," said Emma.

"I love bacon," said Alice with a grin. "And lettuce. And tomato." She gave Emma the tuna sandwich and unwrapped her own. The two girls began to eat, watching shoppers struggle by with bulging supermarket bags, as they made their way towards bus stops and car parks.

"Do you really think Ben likes me?" asked Alice as she chewed on her sandwich.

"I know he does," said Emma. "He even told my mum he does."

"Did he?" said Alice, her eyes wide. "I don't believe it."

"He did. Well, he nodded when my mum asked him if he did."

Alice laughed. "He is nice. I could phone him, or maybe he'll be at the Grove later."

"They'll all be at the Grove. It's the poster competition."

Alice shivered. She suddenly felt cold, despite the sunshine. The memory of what she had done the previous day came flooding back. She could scarcely believe it, and she could scarcely believe that the Grovers would be ready to forgive her. But she had to try.

"I hope you win," she said to Emma.

"No chance," replied Emma. "Mine's terrible. But I'd like to see who does."

They finished their sandwiches and began to walk back towards the Grove. Emma was as nervous as her cousin was. Both girls were deep in their own thoughts, both of them wishing they could just start the last few days all over again.

A dog was barking. Emma turned around and laughed as Wombat came bounding towards them, his tail wagging. Wombat liked Emma, he looked delighted to see her, and Emma was fond of Wombat.

"Hello, Wombat," she said, reaching down to stroke the dog. "Hello, boy." Emma knew that if Wombat had found them, then Stumpy couldn't be far away. "Where's Stum…?"

"Wombat come here!" It was Regina's voice. Emma stopped stroking Wombat and looked up. Regina, Stumpy, Laura, Bradley, Barry and Bill stood a few metres away. Wombat turned his head back in their direction but didn't move. He was panting noisily, his long tongue drooping down from one side of his mouth.

"Tell him, Stumpy," ordered Regina. "Tell him to come here."

Stumpy hesitated. He didn't like it when his friends fell out, and neither did his sister, Laura. But as Stumpy hesitated, Laura felt Regina's fierce glare shift in her direction.

Laura sighed. "You'd better tell him," she said quietly to her brother.

"Wombat," called Stumpy softly. One word was all that was necessary. Stumpy's devoted dog came trotting up and obediently sat by his side.

Emma looked at Alice. Here was her chance. Alice nodded and, with a smile, she walked over to Regina.

"Regina, I just want to say that I'm really..." But Alice had to stop. Regina had turned her back on her. She tried again. "Look, please, Regina, I know what I did..."

"Emma," said Regina loudly, interrupting Alice, "tell your cousin that we're not interested in anything she's got to say." She stared at her friends and, one by one, they also turned away from Alice. Some turned more reluctantly than the others did, but Regina was their leader and eventually Emma and Alice were left gazing at six backs. Finally, even Wombat turned around.

"Regina, please," pleaded Emma. "Alice wants to..."

"We're going to the Grove for the poster competition, Emma," called Regina. "You can come with us if you want to. Just you." She walked away and the others followed. No-one looked back.

"I'm sorry, Alice," whispered Emma after a moment. "I didn't think they'd be like that."

"It's not your fault," said Alice. "Thanks for trying."

"We'll go home," said Emma. "I won't bother with the Grove."

"No, you go. I want you to go. You might have won. I'll go home."

"If you're sure..."

"Of course I am." Alice looked at her cousin and smiled. She reached for her and gave her a hug. "See you later," she said.

• • • • •

Byker Grove was busy and noisy. Grovers waited impatiently in the pool room, in the games room, on the stairs and around the office. Only Sita, Cher and Karen were in the general room. The judges were reaching their decision. The winning poster was being chosen.

Posters on the walls

Regina sat on the stairs, talking to anyone who would listen. "Of course, they won't choose mine, will they? They're bound to ignore mine."

"You've got as much chance as anyone else," said Nikki. "I thought yours was good. Why shouldn't they choose it?"

"Because mine's the only one that's got a great big tear through it. They'll know it's mine and they won't choose it."

Ben was in the corridor. He saw Emma leaning against the stairs and beckoned to her. Emma followed him into the pool room.

"Did you talk to her?" Ben asked.

Emma nodded. "I think she would like to talk to you. She would have been here now but we bumped into Regina and the others earlier, and it didn't go well. Maybe tomorrow."

The poster competition judges had finally chosen the winner. Karen stepped into the corridor. "If you'd all like to come in, we're ready to announce our decision."

Grovers appeared from all over the building. Everyone wanted to know who had won. They filed into the room and sat on chairs and tables. Sita, Cher and Karen were waiting on the stage.

"Right," said Karen. "It's been a very difficult decision and we were really impressed with the standard of the entries."

"Oh, get on with it," said Ollie. "Who's won?"

"We're trying to tell you," answered Sita.

"Shut up, Ollie," said Liam.

Sita continued. "As you know, it was decided that the judges wouldn't know the identity of the artists. That's why all the posters have a number next to them."

"Yeah, yeah," said Ollie. "We know."

"You could have had a look when you were in here on your own," said Bradley. "How do we know someone hasn't paid you to pick their poster?"

"Because we're honest," said Cher. "Do you want to know who's won or not?"

"Yes!" came the shout from a number of Grovers.

"Alright then," said Cher. "The winner is..." She looked at Karen and Sita. They had decided that all three of them would announce the winning number at the same time.

"Poster number... nine," they said together.

Everyone in the room scanned the walls until every eye rested on the winning poster. It was good. The background colour was a vivid blue. On top of that, running from one corner to another, ran a bright yellow, jagged streak that stood out like a flash of lightning. And across the middle of the poster, in shimmering, red letters, the simple message read, 'Don't Waste Energy'.

"Whose is it?" said Regina. "Who did it?"

There was a loud laugh from one corner of the room. "I don't believe it," shouted Nat. "It's mine. It's me. I've won!"

"Oh, no," said Karen.

"Not her," said Cher.

"Oh, dear," said Sita.

"You did it," said Claire to Nat, throwing her arms around her friend.

"Well, I think we can safely say that it wasn't a fix," laughed Ollie to Ben.

"Told you they wouldn't pick mine," said Regina.

"Yeah, but yours was terrible anyway," said Barry.

Nat slid off the table she had been perched on and marched up to the stage. She smiled sweetly at the three judges and then turned to face the other Grovers.

"I'd like to congratulate the judges on their excellent taste," said Nat. "I can see I've made them very happy."

Karen, Cher and Sita did not look very happy. Nat was their old enemy. The last thing they had wanted to do was to choose her poster.

But Nat was enjoying her moment of glory. She couldn't resist one final comment. "And I'm sure the judges will be as delighted as I will to see my poster all over the town." She turned to the judges. "Thank you, girls," she said.

• • • • •

Emma closed the kitchen door, took off her coat and draped it over the back of one of the kitchen chairs. She hadn't enjoyed the session at the Grove.

There were great celebrations after Nat's victory. Emma didn't join in. There were too many looks, too many whispers, and though no-one blamed Emma for what Alice had done, she was her cousin. Most of the Grovers, like Regina, had made it quite clear that they didn't want to see Alice again.

Emma found herself a clean glass from amongst the stack of washing up piled on the draining board. She ran the cold tap, filled the glass and sipped her water. The morning, when it looked for a while as though things might just be getting back to normal, seemed a long time ago. "Oh well, I'd better go up," said Emma.

Alice had cleared a space at the dressing table and was writing on an envelope. She glanced up as her cousin entered the room.

"Who won?"

"Nat," answered Emma. "Bit of a surprise for Karen and the others."

Alice picked up two sheets of notepaper from the dressing table, folded them neatly and slipped them into the envelope. "What time does the last post go?" she asked, licking the envelope and sealing it.

"Not sure," said Emma. "Not yet, anyway."

"Good," said Alice. She took a first-class stamp and stuck it to the envelope. "Will you do something for me?"

"Do something?" Emma asked hesitantly. "What d'you want me to do?"

"Post this," replied her cousin, handing the letter to Emma.

Emma looked at the envelope. It was addressed to Alice's father.

"What is it?" she asked.

"It's a letter to my dad."

"I know that, but why do you want me to post it?"

"Because if I go, I might change my mind at the last minute, and I don't want to do that."

"But what is it? Why are you writing to him? Why don't you just phone?"

"I can't say what I want to say on the phone."

"Alice... what is it? What have you said?"

"If a twelve-year-old like Regina can do it, then so can I."

"Do what?" asked Emma, although she already knew what Alice was about to say.

"I've told my dad I don't want to see him anymore. I can't handle it. It doesn't feel right. I just don't want it anymore."

Emma was horrified. "Alice, it wasn't the same for Regina. She didn't want to see her mum because... because... she wasn't a good mum. She didn't care about Regina. Your dad's not like that. He loves you. And Regina regretted what she'd done. She missed her mum. She wanted to see her again. And she did."

"I haven't said I never want to see him again," said Alice. "I've said, just for now. For a while. Until I feel better about it. I don't know, a year, or two years."

"Two years! Alice, you don't realise what you're doing."

"I do realise," said Alice coldly. "It's my dad's fault that I'm being the way I am. I feel terrible. I know I'm being horrible to everyone but I can't stop myself. I don't want to have to keep thinking about my dad and my mum and Cheryl."

"But Alice, listen…"

"No, Emma, you listen. You don't know what it's like. You don't know what it's like when you just see your dad on Sundays. Eating burgers or going swimming because there's nothing else to do. I'm too old to go swimming with my dad. I know it can never be like it was before, so I don't want to see him. For a while, at least." She held out the envelope to her cousin. "Please post it for me, Emma."

Emma stared. "It's not right," she said softly. "You shouldn't ask me to do it."

"There's no-one else I can ask and I'm too scared to do it myself. But it's what I want. I really do. Please, Emma. Please?"

"But…"

"Please?"

Emma snatched the letter from her cousin's hand, opened the bedroom door and ran quickly down the stairs. She grabbed her coat from the back of the kitchen chair, crammed the envelope into a pocket and hurried out of the house.

"It's not fair," she said as she crossed the road. "She shouldn't have asked me."

Emma began to run. She had taken the letter and now she had to post it, but she wanted it to be over as quickly as possible. She came to the end of the street and turned into the busier main road. Up ahead stood the postbox. Emma had passed it hundreds of times and never even given it a glance. Now it seemed to be waiting for her. She stopped running and walked, but the bright red postbox loomed closer and closer. And then she was there.

She reached into the pocket of her coat, pulled out the envelope and read the name and address written on the front. "It isn't right," she whispered. "She shouldn't have asked me."

Slowly, Emma's hand inched towards the gaping slot in the postbox. The letter touched the metal box. It went into the slot.

YOU CHOOSE DOES EMMA POST THE LETTER?

YES GO TO THE NEXT PAGE

NO GO TO PAGE 80

Emma let the letter go. She heard the envelope tumble down into the darkness and land softly on the jumble of other letters and packages. Emma felt a wave of panic. She wanted to reach down and snatch the letter back. But she couldn't. It was gone. Emma turned away and began to walk home, thinking all the while that in less than an hour the box would be opened and the letter would be on its way to Alice's father. Nothing could stop it now.

"Hello, pet," said Emma's mum, as Emma entered the kitchen. "Where've you been?"

"I... I went to the postbox."

"Postbox? Who've you been writing to, then?"

"It wasn't me, it was Alice. She asked me to post a letter for her."

Emma's mum looked puzzled. "Listen, Emma, I know Alice is upset and emotional just now, but you don't have to run errands for her."

"It's alright," said Emma. "I didn't mind."

"And who was Alice writing to?"

"I... I don't know."

Emma hated telling lies and her mother could see that she was lying. But she could also see that Emma was deeply troubled so she said nothing more. She just gave Emma a long, meaningful look and then went to the freezer, opened the door and took out a large pizza.

Emma watched as her mum switched on the oven and unwrapped the pizza. She knew that piercing look her mother had given her only too well. It could say far more than words.

Emma's mum put the pizza in the oven. "It'll be ready soon," she said. "Go and tell Alice."

Alice was sitting by the bedroom window, staring out into the darkening evening, her face reflected in the glass. Alice looked like her dad. She had always looked like him, ever since she was a baby, everyone said so. And Alice had always been like her dad, too. They had a special understanding of each other. They liked the same things and they laughed at the same things, and often one of them knew what the other one was thinking. They had a secret look they gave each other that only they knew and no-one else ever recognised.

But that was before. Now it seemed to Alice as though her dad never looked at her at all. Not properly. He was too embarrassed. And he certainly didn't understand the way she was feeling.

Alice stared at her own face in the window. It could have been her dad staring back at her. "Why did you do it, Dad?' she whispered.

"Why did you leave us?" Ever since her dad had gone, Alice's feelings had been jumbled and confused. No-one talked to her. No-one explained.

Sometimes she hated her dad for leaving. Sometimes she hated Cheryl and blamed her for making him leave. Sometimes she hated her mum and decided that she was to blame for letting him leave. And sometimes Alice even hated herself and thought that it was all her fault.

"It's no-one's fault," her dad would say. "It just happened."

That's what Alice hated most. When he said that. She didn't believe it. It wasn't true. Nothing just happened. It must have been someone's fault.

The bedroom door opened and Emma came into the room. She sat on her bed.

"Did you post it?" asked Alice, without looking away from the window.

"Of course I did," snapped Emma. "It's what you wanted, isn't it?"

"Yes." Alice stared at her reflection. She could still see her dad's face. "It is what I wanted."

Emma fell back on the bed and gazed up at the ceiling. "Mum says tea'll be ready soon."

Alice wasn't listening. "He'll phone tomorrow, when he gets it. And then he'll drive over. But I don't want to see him."

"You can't stop him from coming."

At last Alice turned away from the window. "But I don't have to be here when he arrives. I'll go out."

"Yeah. And I suppose I'll have to go out with you," said Emma bitterly. She looked at her cousin. "I wish you'd just leave me out of this."

• • • • •

Alice and Emma were sitting at the kitchen table. Neither of them was hungry but Emma's mum had insisted they have breakfast before going out. They picked at their food.

Alice knew that the letter she had written to her dad would have arrived by now. He would have been pleased to see Alice's handwriting on the envelope. He would have opened the letter expecting to read that Alice was having a great time and that she was looking forward to seeing him next weekend. Alice shuddered. She could remember everything she had written. Every sentence. Every word. Last night it had seemed the only answer, but this morning she wasn't so certain.

Emma was thinking about the letter, too, and dreading her uncle's reaction to it. But she also remembered the way she had lied to her mum the previous evening.

Then the telephone rang loudly. Both girls jumped. They looked at the phone and then at each other. Neither of them moved. The phone rang again. And again. And again.

The door to the hallway opened and Emma's mum came into the room. "One of you could have got up and answered it," she said picking up the receiver. "Hello?"

Both girls held their breath, dreading what might come next.

"Oh hello, Jenny," said Emma's mum. "I was going to call you later."

"It's her friend," Emma whispered to Alice. "Come on, let's go out."

The two girls grabbed their coats and went to the back door.

"Hang on, Jenny," said Emma's mum into the telephone. "Make sure you go to the Grove today, Alice," she called as Emma opened the door. "And sort things out."

"We will, Mum," said Emma, closing the door.

The two girls hurried along the path. "I don't even know why we're running away," said Emma. "It's stupid. You wanted this. You'll have to face up to your dad at some time."

Alice didn't answer. They reached the end of the street, turned the corner and walked along the main road. They went past the postbox.

"You did post it, didn't you?" asked Alice.

Emma stopped. "I told you I posted it. You asked me to. You almost begged me to post it. I suppose you've changed your mind about it now."

"No. No, I haven't," said Alice. "It's what I want."

Emma sighed. "So what shall we do? Do you want to try again at the Grove?"

Alice shook her head. "I was thinking of phoning Ben."

"Oh, great," said Emma sarcastically. "You spend the day with Ben.

And what am I supposed to do? Trail around behind you, I suppose."

"No, you go to the Grove," said Alice. "Go and see you're friends. I want you to."

"Yeah, sure."

"Really, Emma, I do. I've caused you enough problems."

The two girls started to walk again. "There's a phone box in the next road," said Emma

• • • • •

At Byker Grove Laura was worried. Her two best friends were Regina and Emma, and recently she had found herself having to choose between the two of them. So far she had chosen Regina, not because she particularly wanted to but because she usually found it easier to go along with what Regina said. But Laura had decided it was time she told Regina she was being unfair to Emma. Deciding to tell her was the easy bit. Actually telling her was more difficult.

They were in the general room where Regina was working on a shopping list for the *Don't Waste Energy Day* party.

"Sausages, burgers," she said as she wrote on her notepad. "I suppose we'll have to get some vegeburgers for people like Nikki. What else?"

Regina hadn't glanced up from her list as she asked the question, but when no answer came she turned to Laura.

"Laura?"

"Yes?" said Laura.

"You're not listening to me, are you?"

Laura took a deep breath. "I was listening. But there's something I've got to say."

"Well, go on, then. I'm not stopping you."

"You might not like it."

Regina put down her pencil. "This is about Emma's cousin, isn't it?"

"No. Well, yes, but it's more about Emma, really."

"What about Emma?"

Laura picked her words carefully. "We were horrible to her when we saw her with Alice yesterday."

"She didn't have to come to the Grove," said Regina. "She could have gone home with her cousin."

"But we should be helping her, instead of making it worse. She's our friend."

Regina opened her mouth to speak but then changed her mind. Laura was right. Regina had seen how dejected Emma had looked during the judging of the poster competition.

She picked up her pencil and returned to her list. "You're probably right. You'll have to try to be a bit nicer to her next time you see her won't you." Regina studied the few items written on the notepad. "Sausages, burgers…" She paused. "We're not having that cousin of hers back here, though."

"But…" Laura stopped. She wanted to say that perhaps the Grovers should give Alice another chance, but at that moment Emma walked into the room.

"Hello, Emma," said Laura brightly. "We were just talking about you."

"Were you?" said Emma.

"Yes," said Regina, beaming at Emma. "I just said to Laura, it's a shame Emma's not here to help us with this list."

Laura stared at Regina.

"List?" asked Emma.

"Yeah," said Regina. "I'm making a list of everything we'll need for the party. Get a chair and you can tell us what you think."

Emma fetched a chair from a corner of the room and joined her friends at the table. "What have you got so far?" she asked.

Before Regina could reply, Bradley came rushing into the room. "Oh, good," he said. "I've been looking for you lot."

"We're busy, Bradley," said Regina. "What do you want?"

"I'm doing a famous old magic trick at the party and I need a volunteer to help me."

"What trick?" asked Emma.

"It's called 'Sawing The Lady In Half'. It'll be fantastic."

The three girls looked at each other, and then at Bradley.

"Go away, Bradley," they said together.

Laura grinned. Things were beginning to get back to normal.

• • • • •

"I'm glad you phoned me," said Ben.

"So am I," replied Alice. "And I'm sorry for the way I've been. I'm not usually like that."

"That's a relief," said Ben.

Alice laughed. She did like Ben. They were wandering through the town, not heading in any particular direction, just walking. They walked in silence for a while. Ben knew there was a lot Alice wanted to say but he had learned from his mistake in the pool room. So he waited.

They came to a low, brick wall at the side of a row of shops and Alice sat down. Ben sat next to her. "I feel terrible," said Alice, without looking at Ben. "For what I did. Everyone at the Grove tried so hard to be nice to me, even Regina, and then I ruined everything. And I don't even know what made me do it, except that..."

"Yeah?" asked Ben.

"I was just so unhappy. I still am. But doing that. Taking the posters. It was so stupid."

"We all do stupid things. I've done some really stupid things."

"Have you? What?"

"Don't ask."

Alice didn't ask, but Ben knew she wanted him to go on.

"You feel angry at people when they let you down. My dad did, and my brother, and my grandad. I went a bit crazy for a while, got into trouble. But Lou Gallagher sorted me out. And my mates. They helped."

Ben paused and thought for a moment. "I don't know if I'm getting this quite right," he continued, "but the thing is, Alice, you have to stop worrying about what you haven't got and just get on with what you have got. I mean, your mum and dad are still around, aren't they?"

Alice nodded.

"And they care about you?"

Alice nodded again.

"Well then, that's a start." Ben stood up. "You just can't expect them to be as sensible as you are," he added with a laugh. "Most of the time, at least."

Alice smiled. "Where are you going?" she asked.

"We're going to the Grove," said Ben.

"But..."

"Come on. Let's get it sorted out."

Alice stood up and they began to walk.

Alice was nervous. The memory of being ignored by Regina and the other young Grovers was still fresh, and the thought of how some of the older members of Byker Grove might react when they saw her again made her feel even more anxious.

"It might not be easy," said Ben as they neared the Grove. "Some of them don't quite see you the way I do."

They reached the long driveway leading up to Byker Grove and Alice stopped. She turned to Ben, leaned forward and kissed him on the cheek. "Thanks, Ben," she said. She looked up towards the Grove and took a deep breath. "This is it," she said, and began to walk up the drive.

Bradley and Barry were lounging by the main doorway. Bradley was moaning to Barry that he still hadn't found a volunteer for his trick of sawing the lady in half.

"They must be worried that I'll get it wrong. Me? The greatest magician in Byker, probably the greatest magician in the whole of Newca..." Bradley stopped as he saw Alice approaching. "Look who's coming," he whispered to Barry.

Barry looked and gave a low whistle. "This could be interesting," he said. The two boys went into the Grove.

Alice and Ben reached the doorway and went inside, just as Nat, Claire and Teraise came out of the office. Alice smiled at them as she walked on towards the general room.

Nat raised her eyebrows and grinned. "Brave," she said, "coming back after what she did. Let's see what happens."

Alice and Ben went into the general room. Regina, Laura and Emma were still sitting at one of the tables. They looked up, but even Regina was too surprised to say anything.

There was no announcement. No-one actually said that Alice had returned with something to say. Everyone seemed to just know. Alice and Ben sat on the edge of the stage and within minutes the room began to fill.

Nat, Claire and Teraise lingered by the drinks machine. Ollie and Liam arrived, still clutching pool cues. Barry, Bradley, Bill, Joe, Stumpy and Wombat soon followed. Nikki and Matt came in just after and went over to where Greg was sitting in his wheelchair. Finally Sita, Karen and Cher swept into the room.

The room was suddenly quiet. Alice swallowed and stood up.

"I think most people are here," she said.

"Most people who matter," said Cher.

"I've got something to say."

"We don't want to hear it," said Regina.

"Ssshh, Regina," said Laura.

"I want to say I'm sorry," said Alice. "Very sorry. I don't know why I did what I did. It was a stupid and horrible thing to do."

The Grovers were silent. Everyone watched Alice, waiting for her to continue. She looked at Regina. "And I'm sorry for tearing your poster, Regina. I honestly didn't mean to do that. It was an accident."

Alice turned to Emma. "And I want to say sorry to my cousin. She's had a terrible time since I got here, and I didn't want that to happen. I didn't want any of this to happen."

Alice felt the tears pricking her eyes but she had to go on. "It's just that... well, recently... things have been a bit... well, a bit..."

The tears were running down Alice's cheeks. No-one moved. No-one spoke. No-one knew what to say. Finally, Nikki stepped forward and took Alice's hands in her own.

It was more than Alice could bear. She pulled away from Nikki and rushed from the room.

Ben broke the tense, uncomfortable silence. "Isn't anyone going after her?"

"What for?" said Nat with a shrug. "She said what she wanted to say. Why should we go after her?"

"Because... because..." Ben strode angrily out through the doorway and into the corridor. "Alice, wait," he called. "Wait!"

"What a hero," said Nat.

Alice had reached the end of the drive when she heard Ben calling. She turned to see him running towards her. She was sobbing; the tears were streaming down her face. Ben didn't know what to do when he reached Alice. He wanted to comfort her. But he didn't know how.

"Oh, Ben," said Alice. "It was terrible."

Ben slowly reached out and took one of Alice's hands in his. He felt Alice grip his fingers tightly. They stood like that for a moment and then Ben found himself putting both his arms around Alice and pulling her gently towards him.

"I was hoping you'd do that," sobbed Alice through her tears. She let her head drop on to his shoulder.

"You were great," said Ben. "You didn't have to run out. You could have stayed. We'll go back in there."

"No, I couldn't. I don't want to."

"But..."

"I can't face them anymore. Not now. Will you walk back to Emma's with me?"

"Yeah, in a minute," Ben answered. He held Alice a little tighter and pulled her a little closer. "We'll go in a minute."

Tina was in the office when she heard Ben shout Alice's name. She heard the shout, she heard Ben running, and then there was silence. Complete silence. And the Grove was hardly ever completely silent.

Tina got up from her desk, went to the door and peered into the corridor. It was deserted. She walked along the corridor and went into the general room. All the Grovers were there but no-one said a word. Some of them looked embarrassed, others looked guilty, and others looked concerned.

"What's going on?" asked Tina.

"Apology time," said Teraise.

"Who from?"

"Emma's cousin. She came in and told us all how sorry she was for what she'd done."

"And she meant it," said Nikki.

"Well, that's good," said Tina. She looked around the room. "And what did you lot do?"

Most of the Grovers avoided Tina's eyes.

"Nothing," said Teraise.

"Oh, that's big of you all. Well done."

"We would have, but..."

"But what?"

"Well, she didn't really give us a chance."

"Look," said Tina. "It's not always easy to say you're sorry. Specially when it's to a whole bunch of people you hardly know."

"She shouldn't have ruined my poster," said Regina.

"No, Regina, she shouldn't," said Tina. "And you've never done anything you shouldn't have, I suppose?"

"I..." For once, even Regina was lost for words.

"Honestly," said Tina, "sometimes I despair of you lot." She walked out, leaving the room as silent as when she walked in.

Regina went to speak but decided against it. Ollie grinned nervously and fiddled with the pool cue he was holding, Stumpy looked at Wombat and stroked his head, while other Grovers looked at the floor or out of the windows.

"She's right." It was Greg who had spoken. "You ought to let her come back. What's the point in carrying it on? There's bigger things to worry about."

"We've got to give her another chance," said Nikki. "She didn't mean to do what she did. And it doesn't matter anymore, anyway."

Everyone began to voice his or her agreement, even Regina. "Yes," she said. "We'll give her another chance. Emma can tell her when she gets home."

"No," said Emma. "I've done enough. Someone else ought to do it. And it'll mean more if it's not me who tells her."

"She's right, it should be someone else," said Sita.

Gradually all eyes in the room turned to Regina.

"Me?" she said.

"Yes, Regina, you," said Teraise.

"But why me?"

"You're the one who wanted her banned."

"We all wanted her banned."

"But it was your poster she tore. It'll be best if it comes from you."

"But..." Regina searched for an excuse to not go. "But... oh... oh, alright, I'll tell her."

• • • • •

Ben and Alice had walked hand-in-hand for more than ten minutes. They walked slowly, neither of them really wanting to reach Emma's house. But they were nearly there. They hadn't spoken very much but Alice was feeling much better. At least she'd done it. She'd found the courage to go back to the Grove and apologise. She didn't expect many of the Grovers to feel better about her but at least she felt better about herself. She suddenly realised that her face must be tear-stained and that her eyes would look puffy and red.

"I bet I look terrible," she said. "I look awful when I cry."

"No," replied Ben with a laugh. "You look alright. You should cry more often. It suits you."

Alice shook her head. "I've cried enough lately. More than enough."

They came to a corner and turned into the road which led to Emma's house. Alice stopped.

"Oh, no!"

"What?" said Ben. "What's the matter?"

"It's my dad," said Alice pointing. "That's his car."

In the trauma and emotion of the last couple of hours Alice had completely forgotten about her letter to her father.

"So?" said Ben. "He's come to see you. What's wrong with that?"

"But you don't understand, Ben. I wrote to him. I told him that all this was his fault. I said I didn't want to see him anymore."

"But why?"

"Regina had told me about splitting from her mum and it… it just seemed the right thing to do. He's come to get me. To take me back."

Ben squeezed Alice's hand tightly and turned her to face him. "Look," he said. "Go in and talk to him. Tell him you're sorry. Explain what's happened. Tell him about today and how you've sorted it out at the Grove. He'll understand."

"Ben, I can't. He'll never forgive me for the things I said."

"He will. Just talk to him. Like you've talked to me."

Alice stared at her dad's car. Why now? Just when it seemed that things were beginning to improve. Why this? The letter. Why did she write it? Why did she ask Emma to post it?

"I don't know what to do, Ben," she whispered. "I can't face him."

"You can," said Ben. "And you've got to."

YOU CHOOSE DOES ALICE FACE HER DAD?

YES GO TO THE NEXT PAGE

NO GO TO PAGE 65

Alice looked at the car again. She nodded. "I've got to. You're right."

She went to walk towards the house but then stopped. "But if he takes me home it means I won't see you anymore."

Ben had already realised what would happen when Alice saw her dad. "Not for now," he said. "But… you could write. Or phone. And maybe next holiday…"

Alice reached out and took both of Ben's hands in hers. She looked into his eyes. "I will see you again, Ben," she said, and leaned forward and kissed him briefly on the lips. Then she turned and ran towards the house.

Ben watched her go. "Just my luck," he whispered.

Alice didn't look back. She ran to the house and along the path to the back door. She reached for the handle and opened the door. Her dad was sitting at the table with Emma's parents.

He looked up as Alice came bursting through the door.

"I'm sorry, Dad," she said. "I'm really sorry."

"No, love," said Alice's dad, as he stood up and wrapped his arms around her. "It's me who's sorry."

Emma's mum turned to her husband. "We'll go and watch the telly for a while. I think your favourite programme's on."

"Is it?" he asked with a puzzled look.

Emma's mum sighed and glanced towards Alice and her dad who were still hugging each other.

"Oh. Oh, yeah," said Emma's dad at last. "Yeah. My favourite programme. Mustn't miss that."

Outside, Ben wasn't sure what to do. He didn't want to go back to the Grove, he was still angry with the others for the way they had treated Alice. But he didn't feel like going home either. He was worried about Alice and wondering what was happening at Emma's house.

He thought of finding a phone box and calling Alice. But it was too soon. Whatever Alice's dad had to say was being said at that moment and Ben didn't want to make the situation more difficult than it already was.

He decided to walk in the direction of the Grove, but to go straight past and walk on into town. He wandered aimlessly, his hands pushed deep into his pockets and his eyes staring down at the pavement.

"Where's Alice?"

Ben looked up to see Regina marching towards him with Emma.

"She's at yours," said Ben, nodding at Emma.

"I've come to tell her that I've convinced the others that we ought to give her another chance," said Regina. "We've forgiven her and we want her to come back."

"Is that right?" said Ben to Emma.

"Something like that," she replied with a frown at Regina.

"Well, you're a bit late. Her dad's there. He's come to take her home."

"Her dad! Oh no, the letter!"

"What letter?" said Regina.

"Come on," said Emma, and she ran off.

Regina looked at Ben and then at Emma as she raced away. She started running after Emma. "What letter?" she called.

• • • • •

"I've never been much good at talking," said Alice's dad.

Alice shook her head.

"It's not that I didn't want to, I just don't find it easy. Not about things that really matter."

"I know you don't, Dad, but you just kept saying 'give it time' and 'we'll have to make the best of it' and I didn't want to give it time and make the best of it. I wanted it to be like it was before."

They were sitting in the kitchen, facing each other and holding hands.

"I phoned your mum after I got your letter."

"I thought you would."

"She was good. Really good. She said when you get back we all ought to sit down and try and talk about it properly."

"What, Cheryl as well?"

Her dad laughed. "No, not Cheryl. Not yet. But maybe, if we give it…"

"Time?" said Alice with a smile.

Her dad returned the smile. "See what I mean?" he said. "About talking? But I will try, Alice. Really, I will."

They were silent for a few moments and Alice realised that she felt closer, then, to her dad than she had for a long time. Since the split-up.

"I didn't mean what I wrote, Dad," she said.

"I know you didn't, love."

"I just couldn't go on pretending everything was normal when I'm with you. It's not. I hardly know Cheryl and you've been… different."

"Have I?"

"Like you're on your best behaviour. And so is Cheryl. And Mum…" Alice's voice trailed off.

"I know it must be difficult for your mum, Alice. I think I understand. I hurt her a lot by leaving. And you."

"That's a start, Dad," said Alice, squeezing her dad's hands.

"What is?"

"It's the first time you've said that. About us being hurt."

Her dad sighed and stood up. "Let's go home, eh, love? Let's go home and make a proper new start."

"I'll go and pack," said Alice, but before she could get off her chair the back door was flung open and Emma and Regina came rushing in.

"It wasn't Alice's fault," gasped Emma. "Not really. She was upset and I posted the letter. I knew she didn't really want to send it. Not really. She was just upset and…"

"Emma!" said Alice's dad loudly.

Emma stopped speaking and stood panting in the doorway, desperately trying to get her breath back. Regina stood next to her, her face bright red. She was even more breathless than Emma.

"You two had better sit down," said Alice's dad with a grin. "Looks like you need a rest."

Emma tried to speak again. "But…"

"It's alright," said Alice's dad. "I know all about it. Alice and I have had a really good talk."

"Oh," said Emma, collapsing on to a chair. "That's alright, then." Regina sat down too; puffing and blowing like a marathon runner.

"Alice and I are going home," said Alice's dad. "We've got a lot of things to sort out."

Regina leapt off her chair. "But she can't go home. We want her to come back. To the Grove. We want her to be friends. With all of us. We want her to help with my saving energy day. And we want her to be at the party."

Alice's dad gazed down at the small girl standing in front of him. "And who are you, then?"

"I'm Regina," said Regina.

"Oh, Regina. The one with the torn poster."

"Yes, but I've forgiven Alice for that," said Regina, nodding furiously. "We all have. And we want her to come back to the Grove. We need her, to help with the party."

"Oh, you need her, do you?"

Regina nodded again. "Please let her come back."

Alice's dad looked at his daughter. He shrugged his shoulders. "What do you want to do, love?"

Alice hesitated. "But you wanted me to come home. To make a new start."

Her dad smiled. "I think I can wait a few more days. It'll give me time to do some thinking. And anyway, I wouldn't want you to miss out on all the things Regina seems to have planned. She needs you."

Alice looked at Regina, then at Emma, and then at her dad. "Alright," she said. "I'll stay."

"Phew," gasped Regina, and she sank back down on her chair.

• • • • •

No-one made a fuss the next day when Alice walked into the Grove with her cousin. Regina had got there early; she was waiting by the front door as Tina drove up in her car to unlock the building. And as each Grover arrived Regina explained everything that had happened on the previous evening.

She told them how she had talked Alice's dad into letting Alice stay. She told them how she had convinced Alice she really ought to stay. And she told them how grateful Alice and her dad were to her for sorting out the whole situation.

"And now," Regina said to Karen, Cher and Sita as she finished her story for at least the tenth time, "we can get on with what's really important."

"And what might that be?" said Karen with a grin.

"My *Don't Waste Energy Day*, of course."

"Oh that," said Karen innocently. "We'd forgotten all about that, hadn't we girls?"

Regina scowled.

Emma and Alice arrived a little later. Alice was nervous, but there was no need to worry. Bradley was the first to greet her. "Nice to see you back," he said.

"Thanks," said Alice.

"Actually, I was hoping to see you," Bradley continued.

"Oh?"

"Yeah. There's a famous magic trick called 'Sawing The Lady In Half' and I'm still looking for a volunteer. I don't know if you'd be interes... No, wait. Wait!"

Alice and Emma had gone. There were friendly faces everywhere. Everyone looked pleased to see Alice. There were smiles and nods and winks and grins. But there was no Ben.

Ben was at home. Ben was in a bad mood. He had stayed in bed until Lou called up the stairs that it was about time he was up. He had dragged himself out of bed, stayed in the bath until the water had gone cold, pulled on some clothes and then slouched down to the kitchen.

Lou was reading a newspaper. "Morning," she said. "Or is it afternoon?"

Ben didn't answer so Lou tried again. "Are you having breakfast or are you going straight for dinner? It's nearly time."

"Very funny," said Ben. "I'm not hungry anyway."

Lou watched Ben go to the fridge, pour himself some orange juice and walk out of the room. "And good morning to you too, Lou," she said.

Ben threw himself down in front of the television and reached for the remote control. He switched from one channel to the next, and the next and the next. There was nothing he wanted to see. He switched to text and read the sports news. Then he switched back to the channel he had started with. He turned up the volume. He turned it down again. He was bored. And fed up.

"Is there something wrong by any chance?" Lou stood in the doorway.

"Wrong? Why should there be?"

"Well, you're a right misery this morning and I don't usually find you watching daytime television."

Ben switched off the television. "It's Alice."

"The girl you told me about?"

Ben nodded. "Her dad came yesterday. He's taken her home."

"Oh. I see."

Lou walked to the sofa and sat by Ben's side. "Come on, then," she said. "Let's hear it."

Lou listened as Ben told her everything that had happened the previous day. She listened in silence, letting Ben tell the whole story. Lou was a good listener. She had to be. Her foster children usually came to her when they were troubled.

Lou waited until Ben had finished. She thought for a moment. "Well, that's that then, Ben," she said.

"But I really like her, Lou."

"I can see that, but it's no use you sitting here brooding about it. She'll write, if she thinks anything of you. And then maybe you'll see her again."

"Yeah, maybe," said Ben.

"Now come on, get yourself off down to the Grove. I don't want you moping around here all day."

"I don't feel like..."

"Off you go," said Lou, giving Ben a friendly shove.

Ben laughed. He hauled himself up from the chair. "See you, Lou," he said.

"Yes, love," she replied. "See you."

Ben walked to the Grove. He felt better for talking to Lou. He always did. But he was still thinking about Alice and wondering where she was and what she was doing as he walked up the drive. He could see many of the Grovers in the grounds. Regina was getting them to build the bonfire. Ben didn't feel like joining in so he went inside the building and straight into the pool room.

Laura saw him go in as she came out of the office. She was about to call out to him but changed her mind. She hurried out through the front door with a wide smile on her face.

Ben was glad to discover there was no-one in the pool room. He didn't particularly want to talk to anyone, and he wasn't in the mood for jokes from Ollie or Liam.

He set up the pool balls, found himself a cue and started to practise. He wasn't really thinking about his game, but slowly he began to concentrate a little bit more on each shot.

Ben leaned over the table, lining up a long shot to the top right-hand pocket.

"I thought you wanted to teach me how to play pool," said a voice from the doorway.

Ben leapt up and turned around. "Alice!" he said.

• • • • •

The next few days passed quickly. The grounds of the Grove were transformed. The huge bonfire was built, a barbecue, tables and benches were set up, and a temporary stage made of wooden planks and crates stood ready for the entertainment.

Cardboard boxes and plastic bags full of food and drink were carried in to the Grove and last-minute rehearsals took place behind closed doors. Bradley had reluctantly accepted that he was never going to find someone willing to be sawn in half, even if it wasn't for real, so he had returned to some of his old magic tricks.

Alice was completely changed. She liked being with Ben but she also enjoyed spending time with her cousin and getting to know some of the older Grovers. And she was particularly nice to Regina. No task was too difficult and no little job was too much trouble. She had a lot of making up to do, and she did it, and in return Regina came to consider that Alice was a special friend of hers.

Don't Waste Energy Day arrived. It was bright and dry, but cold.

"At least it won't rain," Regina told Laura and Barry. "I watched the weather forecast on telly last night."

The Grove was in semi-darkness. Half the lights were switched off and so were the drinks machine and the television. The heating had been turned down, doors were closed and taps were turned firmly off. Many of the Grovers sat around in the general room – feeling miserable.

"Not a lot of laughs, is it?" said Ollie pulling the collar of his coat up around his neck. "Sitting here in the cold, hardly able to see who's sitting next to you."

"Don't exaggerate," said Sita. "We're making a very serious point."

"Oh yeah?"

"Yeah. Regina's right. We take all these things for granted. Just think what it'd be like if we didn't have electricity and gas."

"But we have got it, and I'm freezing," moaned Ollie. "Might as well be outside, it's probably warmer out there. Maybe we should light the bonfire now."

"Don't you dare," said Regina as she marched into the room. "We're setting an example for everyone else to see."

"See? You can't see a thing in here." Ollie looked out through the window as he heard the sound of an approaching vehicle. "Hello, who's this then?"

A van pulled up outside the front door. "Post's arrived, Regina," said Ollie.

"What?"

"The *Byker Post*. That's what it says on the van, anyway."

"It's the posters," yelled Regina, and she rushed from the room.

And it was. The van driver brought out a large, wrapped parcel and carried it into the Grove. Tina produced a pair of scissors and the Grovers crowded round as she cut the cord tied around the package and pulled out the top poster.

It looked even better than Nat's original work. The background blue was more vivid, the yellow flash of electricity was more brilliant and the red lettering stood out and almost shouted: 'Don't Waste Energy.'

Nat grinned. "Not bad," she said. "Not bad at all. Even though I say it myself."

"We're all taking them round the town tomorrow," said Regina. "But we'll put one up in here for now."

She took the poster from Tina and walked towards the nearest wall.

"Regina?" It was Alice.

"Yes?" said Regina.

"Can I do it?"

Regina smiled. "Of course you can, Alice."

• • • • •

"Calls himself a magician? I could do better than that." Ollie didn't think much of Bradley's tricks.

"He is a magician," said Regina, leaping to the defence of her friend. "He's very good. He was nearly good enough to join our group."

"Oh, yeah, you and your lot used to do a bit of magic, didn't you?"

laughed Ollie. "Why aren't you up there with him? He could do with a bit of help."

Regina frowned. "Where d'you think I'd find the time to rehearse magic tricks? Haven't I got enough to do? If it wasn't for me, none of this would be happening."

The party was going well. The bonfire had blazed for more than an hour and was beginning to die down. Candles burned brightly in jars on the tables, and lamps with more candles hung from some of the closest trees.

Ollie and Liam had surprised everyone by offering to be barbecue chefs. And apart from a few blackened sausages, the food had tasted very good.

"At least it was edible," Nat said to Claire as she finished a second burger.

Most of the Grovers sat at benches watching Bradley perform his final trick. Sadly for Bradley there was no sawing involved, but as his magician's cloak swirled around, he put both hands up to his mouth and appeared to pull out a long string of coloured handkerchiefs. The Grovers clapped and cheered as Bradley took a slow and extravagant bow.

"Get off!" yelled Liam with a grin, but even he was secretly impressed.

Bradley swept off the stage and Regina swept on to it.

"Thank you, Bradley," she said. "And now, it's time for our top of the bill act. Let's give a real Byker Grove welcome to Karen, Sita and Cher!"

The Grovers burst into applause as the three girls ran on to the stage. They looked stunning. They were wearing matching dresses in blue, yellow and red, the same colours as on Nat's poster.

"Must be a bit cold in them dresses," whispered Ollie to Liam.

"Yeah, but they look good though, don't they?"

The girls began to sing, and as their sweet harmonies filled the evening air, the grounds of Byker Grove were bathed in firelight and candlelight. Everyone watched and listened in absolute silence as the shadows cast by the bonfire flickered across the stage. At the end of the song every one of the Grovers stood and applauded loudly.

"Thanks very much," said Karen. "We're going to do a slow one now, so if any of you lads fancy asking someone to dance, now's your chance."

The boys hesitated. Going out with someone was one thing, dancing was another, but as Karen, Cher and Sita started their second song, Ben was the first to move.

He went to Alice. "D'you want to dance?"

Alice nodded and they walked to the space in front of the stage. Ben put his arms around Alice's waist, she put hers around his shoulders and they danced slowly to the rhythm of the song.

Liam strode up to Nat. "D'you wanna have a go?"

"Oh, Liam, you've got such a way with words," laughed Nat. "How could I refuse?"

Ollie wasn't going to be left out. He sidled sheepishly over to Claire and asked her to dance. Claire nodded and got up. Bill was next. He asked Laura if she would dance. Laura blushed, but walked with him into the dancing area. Gradually more and more of the Grovers began to dance.

Regina walked over to Bradley. "Do you want to dance?"

"I thought we were supposed to do the asking?" said Bradley.

"I can't wait all night," said Regina. "D'you want to or not?"

Bradley shrugged, nodded and got up to dance with Regina.

Tina watched from the side of the stage. "Ah," she whispered. "It's so romantic."

Ben and Alice were dancing closely.

"What time tomorrow are you going home?" asked Ben.

"In the evening. My dad said he'll come at about seven."

"I'll miss you," said Ben.

"And I'll miss you," replied Alice. "But I'll write to you. And I'll see you again. And we've got tomorrow. I want to help with getting the posters put up."

"Yeah," said Ben. "We've got tomorrow."

The song ended and Ben and Alice kissed.

• • • • •

Regina was handing out posters.

"Take as many as you want," she said to the assembled Grovers who had gathered in the general room the following morning. "There are five hundred posters here. Let's see how many we can get put up by five o'clock."

There were a few embarrassed looks and nudges that morning at Byker Grove. Several new romances had seemed to be developing in the party atmosphere of the previous evening. But now it was down to business. Regina was going to make sure of that.

The Grovers grabbed handfuls of posters and Ollie and Liam were first to head for the door.

"Wait!" called Regina. "We've got to have the photo taken first."

"What photo?" said Ollie.

"For the *Byker Post*. The photographer's in the office talking to Tina."

"Oh. Oh, right," said Liam. "Better hang on, then."

The photographer emerged from the office soon after and he led the Grovers out to the front of the building.

"Right," he said. "We'll have the artist and young Regina crouching down at the front. They can hold one of the posters between them."

Regina and Nat took a poster and crouched down on the front step. The photographer glanced around at the other Grovers. His eyes rested on Karen, Cher and Sita.

"Perhaps you three would like to stand just behind them?"

"Certainly," said Karen with a smile. "Come on girls."

Karen, Cher and Sita walked into position and stood smiling behind Regina and Nat. "Told you they'd want a bit of glamour," said Karen to Nat.

Nat scowled.

"Now the rest of you just gather round them," said the photographer. "Close as you can, but make sure we can see all your faces."

The Grovers huddled together and the photographer looked into his camera. He adjusted the lens on the front and seemed ready to take the photograph. Then he stopped, looked up and turned to Tina who was standing at his side.

"What's that dog doing there?"

"Oh, that's Wombat," laughed Tina. "He's got to be in the photo. He's a member of Byker Grove."

The photographer shrugged. "Fair enough," he said, looking into the camera again. "Right, keep still everyone. Say cheese."

"Cheese!" yelled the Grovers and the camera clicked.

• • • • •

Posters were appearing in shop windows all over Newcastle. The Grovers had worked hard and Alice had worked harder than anyone.

She was determined to do everything she could to make up for her actions of more than a week ago.

"We should have brought more," she said to Ben as they walked out of a shoe shop, having talked the manager into putting a poster in the front window.

"It's not company policy to put posters in our windows," she had told Alice.

"But this is such a worthwhile thing to do," Alice had replied. "It's an important message and you'll be doing a service to the whole community. Your customers will really appreciate it."

"Oh, alright," the manager had said, taking the poster from Alice. "I suppose you're right. I'll do it later."

At that point the manager had expected Alice to leave, but she didn't move. "Why don't you do it now," she'd said with a broad smile. "Just in case you forget."

Alice and Ben stood outside the shop and watched the shop manager tape the poster to the window. Alice waved and shouted her thanks.

"We'll be running out of shops at this rate," said Ben. "We don't have to go in every shop in Newcastle. We can leave some for the others."

Alice smiled. "I just want to do what I can."

"Yeah, I know."

"Right, let's try the shop next door," said Alice.

"Hang on," said Ben. Alice stopped and looked at Ben.

"Look, there's something I've got to do," he said. "Would you mind getting rid of the last few on your own?"

"Oh," said Alice. "Yes. If that's what you want."

Alice felt hurt. It was the last day of her holiday and she wanted to spend as much time as possible with Ben.

"I'll see you later," said Ben brightly. "Back at the Grove. I'll see you before you leave. It's just that it's really important and I've got to do it now."

Alice nodded.

"You're sure you don't mind?" asked Ben.

"No, Ben, I don't mind," said Alice sharply. "I'll see you later, then. Back at the Grove." She walked off towards the next shop.

Ben was grinning as he watched her go.

The last few posters proved difficult to get rid of, mainly because most of the shops already had them. But Alice did it. She refused to give up until they were all gone. And by late afternoon, they were.

Alice caught the bus back to the Grove; she was too weary to walk. She really did feel hurt. Ben could have stayed with her. Surely whatever he had to do could have waited until tomorrow. It couldn't have been that important.

She walked into the Grove and went into the general room. It was crowded. Everyone else seemed to have finished before Alice had, even Regina.

"We wondered when you'd get back," said Emma.

"I wanted to get all the posters put up," said Alice.

"You've done more than anyone else," said Regina. "Thanks."

"I enjoyed it." Alice looked around the room. "Where's Ben?"

"Ben? I don't know," said Regina. "Emma, do you know where Ben is?"

Emma shook her head. "Nikki, have you seen Ben?"

"Ben? No, not since this morning."

No-one knew where Ben was.

"He told me he had something important to do," said Ollie. "Maybe he's not finished yet."

"No," said Alice. "Maybe not." She looked at her cousin. "I'd better be going, then. Got to pack before my dad arrives."

"Yeah, fine," said Emma. "See you at home later, then." Emma turned back to Regina and Laura and they began to chat.

"Oh. Right," said Alice. Alice had expected to see Ben at the Grove. He wasn't there. She had hoped that her cousin would walk home with her but she obviously didn't want to. In fact, no-one appeared to be bothered that Alice was leaving for good.

"Bye then, everyone," she said.

"Bye," came a few half-hearted calls. Some of the Grovers looked up and smiled, others waved but most of them carried on with whatever they were doing.

Alice sighed and turned around. Ben was standing in the doorway. He was grinning and holding a rolled up poster in his hands.

"I told you I had something to do," he said. "We wanted you to have this. To remind you of Byker Grove. And us."

The other Grovers started to laugh and cheer as Ben handed the poster to Alice.

"I thought I'd seen the last one of these," she said as she unravelled the poster.

"Yeah, but that one's different."

And it was. Every member of Byker Grove had signed the poster and written a message.

Even Wombat had left a paw print. Ben's message and signature was in the centre of the poster. He had written: 'Remember, don't worry about what you haven't got and just get on with what you have got – Don't Waste Energy. See you soon. With love, Ben.'

THE END

Alice looked at the car again. She took one step towards it and then stopped. "I can't, Ben. I just can't. The things I said, they were hurtful. Horrible. I can't go in. I won't."

"But… Alice, wait!" It was too late, Alice was already hurrying away. Ben ran after her.

"But what will you do?" he said as they walked quickly along the pavement. "Where will you go?"

"I don't know. Anywhere. I just can't see him."

"But you can't hide from your dad, Alice. It won't work."

Alice didn't answer. They had reached the main road.

"Look, just stop for a minute. Alice, please!" Ben grabbed one of Alice's arms and pulled her to a standstill. She turned towards him and then glanced nervously back down the road.

"He won't be following us," said Ben. "He didn't even know we were outside the house."

"But he'll go looking for me soon. He'll go to the Grove. We said we were going there today."

Ben tried once more. "Go back, Alice. It won't be as bad as…"

"I'm not going back," snapped Alice. "I said I didn't want to see him and I don't."

"You don't mean that."

"I do mean it!"

"Alice, don't be stupid!"

"I am not being stupid!"

They were arguing. Rowing. Just a few minutes earlier they had been walking hand-in-hand, talking softly, thinking that the worst was over. Now they were standing in the street shouting at each other.

Cars and buses hurtled past on the busy road. Pedestrians approached and avoided looking in their direction as they carefully stepped by. Ben and Alice saw and heard nothing. Just each other. They didn't see the police car as it pulled up on the opposite side of the road. They didn't hear the police officer as he got out of the car and crossed the road. But they heard him when he shouted.

"Hey!"

Ben and Alice stopped.

"What's going on?"

Alice saw the police officer and felt a surge of panic. Surely her dad hadn't reported her missing. Not yet. It was still early. He wouldn't be worried yet.

"Well?" said the police officer. "What's all the noise about?"

"We were... we were just talking," answered Ben.

"Talking? I could hear you in my car." The police officer looked closely at Alice. "Have you been crying? Is this lad bothering you?"

"No," said Alice quickly. "Well... yes, I have been crying. But it's not his fault. He's... he's my...."

"I'm her boyfriend," said Ben quickly.

"Are you?" said the police officer. He stared at Ben, then at Alice, and then back at Ben. "Right. Well, go and argue somewhere else then. In private. Go on. And don't let me see you again."

Ben and Alice went to go but before they had taken more than two or three steps the police officer called to Alice again.

"Just a minute, miss."

Alice stopped. Her dad must have reported her missing and the police officer had only just recognised her from the description he had been given. That must be it. She was certain. She turned back.

"Are you sure you're alright?"

Alice nodded. "I'm fine," she said softly. "Really. I'm fine."

"Go on, then," said the police officer with a smile.

They went. Quickly. They didn't speak again until they came to a road junction that Alice didn't recognise.

"Where now?" Alice asked, looking at Ben for the first time since they had walked away from the police officer.

Ben shrugged. "I dunno. I'm just following you."

"Well, you don't have to. If you don't want to help me I'll find somewhere to go. On my own."

Ben stopped Alice before she could walk away.

"Hang on," he said. "I know where we can go. You'd better come with me."

• • • • •

Emma and Regina were nearly back at Emma's house.

"She might not want to come back to the Grove. Not after the way we treated her," said Emma.

"She will," Regina replied, "once she knows I've forgiven her and that we really want her back. And she won't want to miss the party."

"Do you really want her to come back to the Grove, Regina? Really?"

Regina thought for a moment as she walked. "Yes," she said. "She was upset. We all do silly things when we're upset. Even me."

Emma laughed.

"What are you laughing at?" asked Regina, scowling at her friend.

"Nothing," said Emma, smiling sweetly. They came to the corner of the road leading to Emma's house, and just like Ben and Alice had done some time earlier, they came to a halt.

"Oh, no!" said Emma.

"What?" said Regina.

"That car, outside my house. It's her dad's car. Alice's letter!"

"What letter?" said Regina. "What are you talking about?"

"Alice wrote a horrible letter to her dad. She said she didn't want to see him anymore. She got the idea from you."

"Me? I didn't tell her to write to her dad."

"But you told her about splitting from your mum. That's what gave her the idea."

"Oh," said Regina. "I was only trying to help."

"He must have come to take her home. I bet she's packing right now. We're too late. Oh, come on, Regina."

Emma ran past the car and up the path leading to the back door, followed closely by Regina. She pushed open the door and the two girls burst into the kitchen. Emma's mum and Alice's dad were sitting on either side of the table.

"It wasn't Alice's fault," said Emma before either of the adults could speak. "Not really. She was upset and I posted the letter. I knew she didn't really want to send it. Not really. She was just upset and..."

"Emma!" interrupted her mum. "Where's Alice?"

"But... Isn't she here?"

"You can see she isn't here. Why isn't she with you?"

Alice's dad stood up. His face was pale. "Look," he said, "what's happened to Alice? Where is she?"

"I don't know," said Emma, silently blaming herself for not following her cousin when she ran from the Grove. "She came to the Grove this afternoon and..."

"This afternoon?" said her mum. "Why wasn't she with you before then? You left here together this morning."

"She told me to go to the Grove on my own. She wanted to see Ben."

"Ben!" said Alice's dad angrily. "Who's Ben? What's been going on?"

"Calm down, David." Emma's mum took her brother's hand. "And sit down. Ben's alright. He's a good lad." Emma's mum turned to her daughter and Regina. "And you two sit down as well. Tell us exactly what happened. Everything."

The girls sat on the other two kitchen chairs and began to explain what had happened. They explained how Alice had arrived at the Grove to apologise. They explained how they and the other Grovers had listened in silence to her apology. They explained how she had rushed from the room. And they explained how Tina had told them all that they should forgive Alice and ask her to come back to the Grove.

"It's my fault," said Emma. "I should have gone after her."

"No, it's my fault," said Regina. "I shouldn't have told her about my mum."

Alice's dad shook his head. "I should never have let it get like this. I didn't realise. I should have known how she was feeling."

"Yes, David, you should," said Emma's mum. "But there's no point in worrying about that now. We've got to find her."

"We want her to come back to the Grove," said Regina. "We want her to be friends with us. All of us. And we want her to be at the party."

Alice's dad had hardly heard Regina. "Where is she?" he said, looking at his sister. "Why didn't she come back here?"

Emma had been thinking exactly the same thing. She was gazing down at the floor, wondering what could have happened to her cousin.

She looked up. "Maybe she did come back."

"What?" said Alice's dad.

"Maybe she came back and saw your car, Uncle David. Just like me and Regina did. Maybe she saw your car and was too scared to come in. Maybe she went off somewhere."

Alice's dad stared at Emma. "But where? Where would she go?"

• • • • •

"Well, Alice, you've certainly had quite a week, haven't you?"

Alice smiled and sank back against the deep, soft cushions on the old sofa. It was comfortable and comforting. Alice was exhausted; she could have gone to sleep there and then. Ben sat next to her, and opposite, sitting in an armchair, was Lou Gallagher.

Ben had decided to take Alice to his foster home after their row in the street. Lou was a good listener, he told Alice. She could help. She always listened to her foster children when they had problems.

Fortunately, only Lou was at home when they arrived. Ben told her they needed to talk. Lou could see that. She sat them both down and gradually coaxed Alice into telling the whole story. About her parents, about the posters, about the troubles at the Grove and about running away when she had seen her dad's car.

And Lou had listened. She nodded, and sighed, but only spoke when she felt that Alice needed a little encouragement to continue with her story. It was a familiar story, one that Lou had heard many times before.

Alice said that her dad wouldn't talk to her about splitting up with her mum. He couldn't, even when she asked. And her mum couldn't talk to her either; she was still too upset. So no-one talked to her. No-one explained.

"Do you know, Alice," said Lou when Alice finished her story, "I get far more angry with parents than I ever do with any of my foster kids. People are supposed to get wiser as they get older, but I don't see that very often."

"I don't understand why it happened, Lou," Alice said softly. "I just want to understand."

Lou studied the face of the young girl. She looked so tired, her eyelids were drooping.

"Alice," she said, "you know your dad will be worried about you by now, don't you? You've been here for quite a while."

Alice nodded.

"You ought to phone him, at least."

"But I can't, Lou. Not now. I'm so tired."

"Will you let me call him?"

Alice hesitated; she knew her dad would be worried. "Yes," she said.

"Come with me, Ben," said Lou. "You know Emma's number."

Ben had listened in silence throughout Alice's story. He took one of Alice's hands in his. "Will you be alright?"

"Of course she'll be alright," said Lou with a smile. "Come on."

Ben squeezed Alice's hand and got up and went out of the room with Lou. Alice leaned back on the sofa. Would she be alright? Would it ever be alright again? Would life ever get back to normal, or even something like normal? She couldn't remember what normal was anymore.

Alice was so tired. But she was glad to have talked with Lou. She liked her. Ben had said, on the way there, that Lou would understand. And Ben had been right. Alice liked Ben, too. A lot. The room was warm and the sofa was soft. Alice felt her eyes close and in less than a minute she was asleep, and for the first time in weeks, or even months, there were no bad dreams.

She thought she was dreaming when she felt someone gently shaking her shoulder. Then she heard a voice, calling to her softly. "Alice." She shifted slightly on the sofa but she didn't want to wake up. The voice called again. "Alice." She opened her eyes and, for a moment, had no idea where she was. Lou was smiling down at her.

Alice blinked and tried to clear her mind. She was at Lou's. With Ben. The phone call. She remembered the phone call to her dad.

"Did you speak to him?" she asked anxiously.

"About an hour ago," said Lou.

"An hour? But..."

"You were asleep and I didn't like to wake you."

"But my dad..."

"It's alright. We had a long chat, a very long chat."

"How was he?"

"He's..." Lou chose her words carefully, "a bit... bruised."

Alice sat up and rubbed her eyes. "Bruised?" she said, not quite understanding what Lou meant.

Lou came and sat by Alice's side. "When something like this happens, love, everyone gets bruised. The people who do the leaving and the people they leave behind. And you know that bruises sometimes take quite a while to disappear, don't they?"

Alice smiled and nodded. "Yeah," she whispered.

"I don't know who was right and who was wrong when your dad left your mum," Lou continued. "That's for them to sort out. But I do know they've got to talk to you about it. I think your dad realises it, too. He says he wants to talk."

Alice remembered the letter. "I bet he does," she said.

"Oh, don't worry about the letter. He knows you didn't mean what you said."

Alice looked at Lou. She'd thought she couldn't cry any more after the upset and trauma of the day, but she felt more tears coming to her eyes. "I didn't mean it, Lou," she sobbed. "I just want my dad back."

Lou put one arm around Alice and hugged her. "You'll get your dad back, love," she said. "I'm sure of that."

Alice felt safe wrapped in Lou's big, warm arms. She didn't want to move. But she remembered Ben. "Where's Ben?" she asked.

"He's gone to bed, love. I think he's almost as exhausted by all this as you are."

"I suppose I'd better go back to Emma's now," said Alice.

"Not tonight," Lou answered. "You're staying here."

Alice sat up and stared at Lou.

Lou smiled. "It's fine with your dad and I've already got the spare room ready."

"Oh, Lou… thanks."

"You're dad's gone home and he's left some money with your auntie for you to get the train back tomorrow. If you want to."

"If I want to?"

"He says it's up to you. He'll understand if you want to stay longer. You can talk when you get home."

"But why should I want to stay?"

"Because apparently the kids at Byker Grove want you to stay. They sent young Regina and Emma to tell you."

Lou got up from the sofa. "But you can worry about that tomorrow. Come on, let's get you off to bed."

Alice trailed wearily behind Lou, up the stairs and into the spare room. Five minutes later, she was asleep.

• • • • •

Regina had returned to Emma's house. It was early, and Emma and her parents were still eating breakfast. Regina glanced impatiently at the kitchen clock. After the excitement of the previous evening Regina had decided that only she could convince Alice to stay.

"I thought she'd be back by now," she said.

"Regina, it's not even nine o'clock," said Emma. "She's on her way. She phoned from Ben's."

"Staying at Ben's!" Regina could hardly believe it. "What'll they say at the Grove?"

"I think quite enough has been said at the Grove, don't you Regina?" said Emma's mum. "And I don't want a fuss made when she gets back. Whether or not she stays is her decision. It's up to her."

She got up from the table, carried some of the breakfast things over to the sink and peered out through the window. It was raining hard.

"It's pouring," she said. "I hope Lou's given them an umbrella."

Lou had given them an umbrella. Alice and Ben were on their way. They huddled close together under the large canopy and walked, heads down, through the downpour. Alice didn't mind the rain. She didn't feel like talking. Not yet.

She had woken early, when it was still dark outside. The memories of the day before came flooding back. She listened to the sound of raindrops against the window and relived everything. The whole painful day. And she thought about the decision she still had to make.

The darkness gradually faded as the morning light slowly filtered through a chink in the curtains. Alice gazed around the unfamiliar room and tried to imagine the other young people who had slept there before her. Lou's foster children, probably all of them in far more difficult situations than she.

At last Alice heard the sounds of movement about the house. Doors opening and closing, footsteps on the stairs and then muffled voices from the kitchen below. When she was certain that everyone was up, she dressed quickly, went to the bathroom and then hurried downstairs.

Ben and Lou were alone. Lou had suggested to her husband and her other foster children that they went out.

"Morning, love," said Lou. "Sleep alright?"

Alice nodded. "Yes, thanks."

"Breakfast?"

Alice shook her head. "I think I'd better get back."

"Good idea. It's pouring with rain out there. Take an umbrella. Ben can bring it back."

Lou waved goodbye to Alice on the doorstep after hugging her and telling her that she could return whenever she wanted, and then Ben and Alice set out on the journey back to Emma's. They walked in silence.

They were almost there. Ben had to know. "Are you staying?"

Alice stopped and looked at Ben. The rain hammered against the umbrella. "Ben, I'm sorry. Can we wait? Just till we get back?"

Ben nodded and they began to walk again.

At Emma's house, Regina was rapidly losing patience. "They should be here by now. I've got things to do at the Grove."

"You don't have to wait, Regina," said Emma. "We can manage."

Regina gave Emma a look that said she should know perfectly well that they couldn't possibly manage without her.

"You don't have to wait at all," said Emma's mum, looking out through the window. "They're here."

And they were. The back door opened and Ben and Alice came in, looking wet and bedraggled.

"I'm sorry," said Alice, as she and Ben took off their coats and little puddles of water began to appear all over the kitchen floor.

"Don't worry about that," said Emma's mum. "We're all just delighted to see you."

Regina couldn't wait any longer. "Yes, we are," she said. "And we want you to know that everything's alright now and that we want you to come back to the Grove and that…"

"Regina," said Alice.

"Yes?"

"Thanks. It's really good of you to say that after everything I did." Alice paused and smiled at Ben before going on. "But I've decided to go home. I want to see my dad, and my mum."

"Oh," said Regina.

"Oh," said Emma.

"Oh," said Ben.

• • • • •

The rain cleared the following day, and by the time *Don't Waste Energy Day* arrived the weather was bright and dry. But cold.

"It won't rain," Regina told Laura and Barry at the Grove. "I watched the weather forecast on telly last night."

The Grove was in semi-darkness. Half the lights were switched off and so were the drinks machine and the television. The heating had been turned down, doors were closed and taps were turned firmly off. Many of the Grovers sat around in the general room – feeling miserable.

"Not a lot of laughs, is it?" said Ollie, pulling the collar of his coat up around his neck. "Sitting here in the cold, hardly able to see who's sitting next to you."

"Don't exaggerate," said Sita. "We're making a very serious point."

"Oh yeah?"

"Yeah. Regina's right. We take all these things for granted. Just think what it'd be like if we didn't have electricity and gas."

"But we have got it, and I'm freezing," moaned Ollie. "Might as well be outside, it's probably warmer out there. Maybe we should light the bonfire now."

"Don't you dare," said Regina as she marched into the room. "We're setting an example for everyone else to see."

"See? You can't see a thing in here." Ollie looked out through the window as he heard the sound of an approaching vehicle. "Hello, who's this then?"

A van pulled up outside the front door. "Post's arrived, Regina," said Ollie.

"What?"

"The *Byker Post*. That's what it says on the side of the van, anyway."

"It's the posters," yelled Regina, and she rushed from the room.

And it was. The van driver brought out a large, wrapped parcel and carried it into the Grove. Tina produced a pair of scissors and the Grovers crowded round as she cut the cord tied round the package and pulled out the top poster.

It looked even better than Nat's original work. The background blue was more vivid, the yellow flash of electricity was more brilliant and the red lettering stood out and almost shouted: 'Don't Waste Energy.'

Nat grinned. "Not bad," she said. "Not bad at all. Even though I say it myself."

"We'll be taking them round the town tomorrow," said Regina.

"But we'll put one up in here for now."

Regina took the poster from Tina's hands and walked towards the nearest wall.

• • • • •

"Calls himself a magician? I could do better than that." Ollie didn't think much of Bradley's tricks.

"He is a magician," said Regina, leaping to the defence of her friend. "He's very good. He was nearly good enough to join our group."

"Oh, yeah, you and your lot used to do a bit of magic, didn't you?" laughed Ollie. "Why aren't you up there with him? He could do with a bit of help."

Regina frowned. "Where d'you think I'd find the time to rehearse magic tricks? Haven't I got enough to do? If it wasn't for me none of this would be happening."

The party was going well. The bonfire had blazed for more than an hour and was beginning to die down. Candles burned brightly in jars on the tables, and lamps with more candles hung from some of the closest trees.

Ollie and Liam had surprised everyone by offering to be barbecue chefs. And apart from a few blackened sausages, the food tasted very good.

"At least it was edible," Nat said to Claire as she finished a second burger.

Most of the Grovers sat at benches watching Bradley perform his final trick. Sadly for Bradley there was no sawing involved, but as his magician's cloak swirled around, he put both hands up to his mouth and appeared to pull out a long string of coloured handkerchiefs. The Grovers clapped and cheered as Bradley took a slow and extravagant bow.

"Get off!" yelled Liam with a grin, but even he was secretly impressed.

Bradley swept off the stage and Regina swept on to it.

"Thank you, Bradley," she said. "And now, it's time for our top of the bill act. Let's give a real Byker Grove welcome to Karen, Sita and Cher!"

The Grovers burst into applause as the three girls ran on to the stage. They looked stunning. They were wearing matching dresses in blue, yellow and red, the same colours as on Nat's poster.

"Must be a bit cold in them dresses," whispered Ollie to Liam.

"Yeah, but they look good though, don't they?"

The girls began to sing, and as their sweet harmonies filled the evening air, the grounds of Byker Grove were bathed in firelight and candlelight. Everyone watched and listened in absolute silence as the shadows cast by the bonfire flickered across the stage. At the end of the song every one of the Grovers stood and applauded loudly – everyone but Ben.

Ben wasn't in a party mood. Ben was missing Alice. He'd been missing her all week, ever since she'd gone home. He had tried to talk her into staying but Alice's mind was made up. She had to go home.

Ben had travelled in the car with Alice and Emma's parents to the station, and after Alice said goodbye to her aunt and uncle, he walked with her to the carriage.

At the door they hugged and Alice whispered to Ben. "I'll see you again, Ben, I promise. But I have to go home. I've got to sort things out with my dad. You do understand, don't you?"

Ben looked into Alice's eyes and nodded. And then they kissed.

Ben was thinking of that kiss as the cheers and applause echoed around the grounds of Byker Grove.

"Thanks very much," said Karen. "We're going to do a slow one now, so if any of you lads fancy asking someone to dance, now's your chance."

The boys hesitated. Going out with someone was one thing, dancing was another, but as Karen, Cher and Sita started their second song, Bill marched bravely up to Laura.

"Wanna dance?" he said. Laura blushed, but walked with Bill to the space in front of the stage. They put their arms around each other and began to dance.

Liam strode up to Nat. "D'you wanna have a go?"

"Oh, Liam, you've got such a way with words," laughed Nat. "How could I refuse?"

Ollie wasn't going to be left out. He sidled sheepishly over to Claire and asked her to dance. Claire nodded and got up. Gradually more and more of the Grovers began to dance.

Regina walked over to where Bradley was sitting. "Do you want to dance?"

"I thought we were supposed to do the asking?" said Bradley.

"I can't wait all night," said Regina. "D'you want to or not?"

Bradley shrugged, nodded and got up to dance with Regina.

Ben watched from the shadows, away from the dancing area.

"Romantic, isn't it?"

Ben turned. He hadn't even heard Tina approaching. He shrugged.

"Don't worry, love," said Tina. "You'll see her again."

"Will I?" said Ben, looking at Tina.

"Of course you will. How could she resist a handsome lad like you?"

Ben smiled, and blushed.

• • • • •

"We've got to have our photo taken before we start taking the posters around town," said Regina. "So don't go yet."

It was the following morning and the Grovers had gathered in the general room. There were a few embarrassed looks and nudges that morning at Byker Grove. Several new romances seemed to develop in the party atmosphere of the previous evening. But now it was down to business. Regina was going to make sure of that.

"What photo?" enquired a bleary-eyed Ollie.

"For the *Byker Post*. The photographer's in the office talking to Tina."

"Oh. Oh, right," said Liam. "Better hang on, then."

The photographer emerged from the office soon after and he led the Grovers out to the front of the building.

"Right," he said. "We'll have the artist and young Regina crouching down at the front. They can hold one of the posters between them."

Regina and Nat took a poster and crouched down on the front step. The photographer glanced around at the other Grovers. His eyes rested on Karen, Cher and Sita.

"Perhaps you three would like to stand just behind them?"

"Certainly," said Karen with a smile. "Come on girls."

Karen, Cher and Sita walked into position and stood smiling behind Regina and Nat. "Told you they'd want a bit of glamour," said Karen to Nat.

Nat scowled.

"Now the rest of you just gather round them," said the photographer. "Close as you can, but make sure we can see all your faces."

The Grovers huddled together and the photographer looked into his camera. He adjusted the lens on the front and seemed ready to take the photograph. Then he stopped, looked up and turned to Tina who was standing at his side.

"What's that dog doing there?"

"Oh, that's Wombat," laughed Tina. "He's got to be in the photo. He's a member of Byker Grove."

The photographer shrugged. "Fair enough," he said, looking into the camera again. "Right, keep still everyone. Say cheese."

"Cheese!" yelled the Grovers, and the camera clicked.

A few minutes later, they were back in the general room and Regina began distributing the posters.

"Take as many as you want," she said as the Grovers formed up in a ragged line. "There are five hundred posters. Let's see how many we can get put up by five o'clock."

Ben watched as the others collected their posters and began to move off.

"Coming with us, Ben?" called Ollie as he and Liam walked to the door.

"I'll catch you up later," said Ben.

He waited until everyone had gone and then went over to the, now much smaller, pile of posters. He took one from the top.

• • • • •

Alice stepped out of the car and closed the door.

"I'm really glad you're staying over," said her dad. "You're sure you don't mind sleeping on the sofa?"

"Of course I don't," said Alice.

"It'll be easier when me and Cheryl have got a proper..." He stopped and looked at his daughter. She was smiling. "Whoops," said her dad returning the smile. "Come on, let's get in."

Alice carried her overnight bag and a long cardboard tube. She followed her dad through the front door and up a flight of stairs to the first floor flat. Her dad's girlfriend, Cheryl, was waiting inside.

"Hello, Alice," she said with a smile.

"Hello," Alice replied, dumping her bag on the floor and joining Cheryl on the sofa.

"What's that you've got there?" asked Cheryl, indicating the cardboard tube.

"It's a poster. I brought it to show you and Dad."

Alice pulled the rolled 'Don't Waste Energy' poster from the tube. "Ben sent it."

"I can see that," said her dad with a grin. Underneath the slogan was written: 'See you soon. With love from Ben.'

"The famous Ben. I never got to meet him."

"But you will, Dad. Sometime."

Her dad nodded. "So what are you going to do with your poster?"

"It's going on my bedroom wall with the others. But I wanted you to see it. Both of you."

Alice rolled up the poster and put it back into the tube. "Dad," she said, "I was writing a letter to Ben when you came to collect me. Can I finish it so I can get it in the post?"

"Yeah," said her dad. "Do it in the kitchen, we're a bit cramped for space in here."

Alice went through to the small kitchen and sat at the table. She read the letter she had written to Ben. It was almost finished, she had even signed it: 'With love, Alice.' But she had been thinking about the PS. that she wanted to write at the bottom of the page.

She took out a pen and wrote: 'PS. Tell Lou I think the bruises are starting to fade. She'll know what I mean. XXX'

THE END

Emma stopped. She couldn't let go. She couldn't bear the thought of Alice's dad receiving the letter. Or of what would follow. Her fingers tightened their grip on the envelope and she pulled it back out of the postbox.

She looked at the envelope again. What should she do now? Destroy the letter? Tear it up and throw away the pieces? But she couldn't do that either. She would keep it. Hide it. When Alice calmed down she'd realise it had been a stupid idea to write the letter. Then Emma would tell her she hadn't posted it. And Alice would thank her. Wouldn't she?

Emma stuffed the letter back into her pocket and turned to walk home.

"Hello, pet," said Emma's mum as Emma entered the kitchen. "Where've you been?"

"I… I went for a walk."

"A walk? You don't usually go for walks."

"I wanted to get away from Alice for a while."

Emma's mum looked closely at her daughter. "Did you go to the Grove today? Did Alice sort things out?"

Emma shook her head "We did try, Mum. We were going to. But then we met Regina and some of the others in town." She paused.

"And?" said her mother.

Emma told her mum about the way Regina and her friends had ignored Alice when she tried to apologise.

"Well, she'll just have to try again tomorrow," said Emma's mum. "Regina's not the only person at the Grove. She's not in charge."

Emma smiled. "Sometimes she thinks she is." She watched her mum go to the freezer, open the door and take out a large pizza.

"I'll do this for tea," she said. "Go and tell Alice it'll be ready soon."

Alice was thinking about her dad. They had always been close, so close that often one of them knew what the other one was thinking. They seemed to share the special understanding that dads and daughters sometimes have. They were so alike, in their looks and in their ways. They liked the same things and they laughed at the same things, and they had a secret look they gave each other that only they knew and no-one else ever recognised.

But that was before. Now it seemed to Alice as though her dad never looked at her at all. Not properly. He was too embarrassed. And he certainly didn't understand the way she was feeling. Ever since he had moved out Alice's feelings had been jumbled and confused. And her dad wouldn't talk about it. Neither would her mum. No-one talked to her. No-one explained.

That was why she had written the letter to her dad. It wasn't special anymore between them. There was someone else now. Cheryl. Sometimes she hated Cheryl for taking her dad away, sometimes she hated her dad for leaving, sometimes she hated her mum for letting him leave, and sometimes Alice even hated herself and thought it must be her fault that her dad had gone.

"It's no-one's fault," her dad would say, if ever she asked. "It just happened."

That's what Alice hated most. When he said that. She didn't believe it. It wasn't true. Nothing just happened. It must have been someone's fault.

She had been so angry when she wrote the letter. If he wouldn't listen when she tried to talk to him then what else could she have done? But her anger gradually passed. Now she felt sad, and a little afraid. Not to see her dad. Did she really want that?

The bedroom door opened and Emma came into the room. She went straight to her bed and sat down. She didn't look at her cousin.

"Did you post it?" asked Alice.

Emma didn't answer. She lay back on the bed and turned away from Alice. She could feel her face going red with embarrassment.

"Did you?" demanded Alice.

"Yes, I posted it," lied Emma. "It's what you wanted, isn't it?"

"Yes," answered Alice softly. "It's what I wanted."

Emma couldn't look at her cousin. She stared at the posters on her bedroom walls. "Mum says tea'll be ready soon," she mumbled.

• • • • •

Alice and Emma were sitting at the kitchen table. It was the following morning. Neither of them was hungry but Emma's mum had insisted they have breakfast before going out. They picked at their food.

Alice knew that the letter she had written to her dad would have arrived by now. He would have been pleased to see Alice's handwriting on the envelope. He would have opened the letter expecting to read that Alice was having a great time and that she was looking forward to seeing him next weekend. Alice shivered. She could remember everything she had written. Every sentence. Every word.

Emma was thinking about the letter, too. It was still in her coat pocket. There had been no opportunity last night to take it out and hide it.

Then the telephone rang. Loudly. Both girls jumped. They looked at the phone and then at each other. Neither of them moved. The phone rang again. And again. And again.

Alice was certain that it was her dad and Emma was certain that it wasn't, unless of course he just happened to be ringing for a chat with Alice. Then what would happen?

The door to the hallway opened and Emma's mum came into the room. "One of you could have got up and answered it," she said picking up the receiver. "Hello?"

Both girls held their breath, dreading what might come next.

"Oh hello, Jenny," said Emma's mum. "I was going to call you later."

Emma leaned closer to Alice and whispered. "It's her friend. Come on, let's go out."

The two girls grabbed their coats and went to the back door.

"Hang on, Jenny," said Emma's mum into the telephone. "Make sure you go to the Grove today, Alice," she called as Emma opened the door. "And sort things out."

"We will, Mum," said Emma. She closed the door and they hurried along the path and out on to the pavement. They reached the end of the street, turned the corner and walked along the main road, passing the postbox.

"You did post it, didn't you?" said Alice, half hoping that her cousin would say that she still had the letter.

But Emma didn't know that. The letter was in her pocket and she desperately wanted to tell Alice that she still had it. She stopped and looked at her cousin. Alice was staring at her, anxiously, almost accusingly.

"I told you I posted it," snapped Emma. "You wanted me to post it. You more or less begged me to post it. You haven't changed your mind now, have you?"

Alice hesitated. "No. No, I haven't," she said. "I'm glad you posted it."

Emma looked at her cousin. Was she glad? Really? She didn't look glad. Perhaps she had changed her mind and regretted writing the letter. Emma reached into her pocket and touched the envelope. She wanted to pull it out and give it to Alice and then watch her tear it into a hundred pieces. All she needed from Alice was a word, or even a look. But there was nothing.

Emma took her hand from her pocket with a sigh. "So what shall we do? Do you want to try again at the Grove?"

Alice shook her head. "Not yet. I can't face it yet."

"Well what, then?" said Emma. "We can't spend another day wandering around town."

"You go to the Grove," said Alice. "I'll come later, when I've thought about what I'm going to say."

"But I can't just leave you."

"Yes, you can. I'll be fine. Go and see your friends."

"But…"

"Really, Emma, I want you to. I've caused you enough problems."

Emma nodded. "Alright," she said. "I'll see you later. Bye."

The two girls drifted slowly away in opposite directions, both of them wishing they could have found the courage to admit what they were really thinking.

Alice wandered into town. She couldn't stop thinking about the letter. Last night it had seemed the only answer, but this morning she wasn't so certain. She had wanted to hurt her dad, like he hurt her. She thought again and again about the words she'd written. It wasn't true. She did want to see her dad. She couldn't bear the thought of not seeing him. She loved him.

By the time Alice reached the town centre she had made her decision. She searched quickly for the shop she was looking for and hurried inside.

• • • • •

Emma was glad to be back at the Grove. She hadn't enjoyed being there on the previous afternoon when the poster competition was judged. The posters reminded everyone of what Alice had done and Emma felt embarrassed and self-conscious.

But today was different. Today it seemed almost like any other day at the Grove. No-one stared when Emma arrived, or whispered as she walked past. The Grovers were getting on with what they usually did or were preparing for the *Don't Waste Energy Day* and party. It was almost as though the Grovers had forgotten all about Alice.

Emma was sitting in the general room with Regina and Laura. They had been pleased to see her when she arrived and Regina asked her to come and help them with a shopping list they were making for the party.

No-one mentioned Alice, but every few minutes, as they thought of more and more items to add to the list, Emma would glance over to the doorway, knowing that her cousin could arrive at any minute. Regina didn't notice each time Emma looked up, but Laura did.

"I think I'd better ask Tina how much we can spend," said Regina. "Hang on a minute."

She got up from her chair and went out of the room.

Laura took her chance to question Emma. "Where's Alice?" she asked quietly.

"I'm not sure," said Emma. "I think she'll be here soon. She wants to apologise."

"I wondered why you kept looking at the door."

Emma moved closer to Laura. "Do you think they'll give her another chance, Laura?"

Laura shrugged. "I don't know about everyone else but Regina doesn't want her back."

"But it's not just down to Regina is…" Emma stopped. Regina had returned.

"What's not just down to Regina?" she asked.

"Nothing," said Emma. "It doesn't matter."

"If you're talking about that cousin of yours, then no-one wants her back at the Grove. It's not just me. Is it Laura?"

Emma and Regina looked at Laura. She didn't answer. She couldn't. She hated choosing between her friends. She looked down at the shopping list that was still on the table.

Emma stood up. "Everyone makes mistakes sometimes, Regina," she said, and she walked out of the room.

Regina watched her go and then sat down. "Tina wasn't in the office," she said. "We'll talk to her later."

Laura looked up from the list. "Emma's our friend, Regina," she said. "This must be awful for her. We should be helping her instead of making it worse."

But Regina wasn't listening. "How many burgers do you think we'll need?" she asked.

Emma was standing by the entrance door of Byker Grove, more angry at herself than at Regina. Regina could be infuriating but Emma wasn't surprised at what she had said. And she didn't really blame her for the way she felt about Alice.

Emma stepped through the door and looked down the drive. There was no sign of Alice. Emma wanted her to arrive and get it over with, whatever happened. She looked at her watch. It was already getting late. Alice should have been there by now.

Emma wandered into the grounds and round to the back of the Grove. She sat on the climbing frame. She could still see part of the drive from there. She'd see Alice when she eventually turned up.

"Hi, Emma."

Emma turned and saw Nikki approaching. She had walked through the gate that separated her back garden from the grounds of Byker Grove and had spotted Emma sitting alone on the climbing frame.

"Are you alright?" she said, sitting next to Emma.

"Yeah, I suppose so," answered Emma with a sigh.

"Where's your cousin?"

"I don't know. She's supposed to be coming here. To apologise."

"Oh," said Nikki.

They sat in silence. Emma desperately wanted to tell someone about the letter that was still in her pocket. Nikki was older than most of her other friends and at that moment Emma needed a friend she could talk to.

"Nikki," she said slowly. "Can I tell you something?"

Nikki nodded. "Yeah. If you want."

Emma spoke quickly. She told Nikki how she had returned home on the previous evening to find Alice with the letter she had written to her dad. She told Nikki what Alice had written and how she had pleaded with her to post the letter.

"She kept on and on at me," said Emma. "She almost begged me, so in the end I took it and ran to the postbox."

"And you posted it?" asked Nikki.

Emma reached into her pocket and pulled out the now crumpled envelope.

"She thinks I did. I told her I did. But I couldn't."

Nikki stared at the envelope. "I think you did the right thing."

"Do you?" said Emma. "Really?"

"Yeah, I do, really," answered Nikki.

"But what do I do now?"

"Listen, Emma, you know you asked me if I'd talk to Alice?"

Emma nodded.

"Well, I wasn't sure. But I will, if you still want me to."

"Oh, Nikki, I do," said Emma. "Thanks."

"Come on," said Nikki, "let's go and wait for her inside."

They stood up and wandered back towards the building but as they went to go inside Bradley came through the doorway.

"Oh, great," he said. "I've been looking for you."

"What d'you want, Bradley?" said Nikki.

"Well, I'm doing a famous old magic trick at the party and I need a volunteer to help me."

"What famous old magic trick?" asked Emma.

"It's called 'Sawing The Lady In Half'. It'll be fantastic."

Emma and Nikki looked at each other, and then at Bradley.

"No way," said Nikki, and they walked into the building.

They waited until the end of the session but Alice didn't turn up.

"I suppose she couldn't do it," said Emma. "She must have gone home. I'm not really surprised."

"D'you want me to come back with you?" asked Nikki.

Emma smiled and nodded.

Alice was at home. Emma and Nikki saw the bedroom light on as they approached the house.

"I just hope my mum's not in," said Emma. "Alice told her she'd go to the Grove today."

They went in through the back door. Emma's mum was not at home and neither was her dad. Emma led the way up the stairs.

She opened the bedroom door and saw Alice. She look excited, happy, and began speaking to Emma before she had even noticed Nikki. "Emma, I've been waiting for you to get back. I wanted to tell you… Oh." Alice stopped as Nikki followed Emma into the room.

"Hi, Alice," she said.

"Hello," Alice replied. She didn't seem very pleased to see Nikki.

"Nikki's come to talk," said Emma.

"Talk? What about?" said Alice, her smile rapidly fading.

"Well, her mum and dad split up too. We thought it might help."

"I don't need any help," said Alice irritably. "Not now."

Emma was growing concerned. "What have you done, Alice?"

Alice hesitated. "I… I can't really say in front of Nikki."

"You mean the letter?" said Emma. "I've told Nikki about the letter."

"What?"

Nikki was beginning to feel uncomfortable. "Look, maybe I should go," she said.

"No. Stay here, Nikki," said Emma.

"You shouldn't have said anything," snapped Alice angrily. "You did that before, even before I'd got here, and I told you I didn't want you talking about me to other people."

"I had to tell someone."

"She was worried about it, Alice," said Nikki.

For a moment it seemed as though Alice would turn on Nikki. But she stopped herself. She smiled. "Oh, well, it doesn't really matter. Not now. But you shouldn't have said anything, Emma."

She sat on her bed and Emma sat next to her.

"Alice, what have you done?"

"After I left you today I went into town. I was thinking about my dad. I realised I shouldn't have written the letter. I do want to see him. I do need to talk to him. I was going to phone."

Emma and Nikki exchanged anxious looks. "But you didn't, did you?" asked Emma.

"No. I didn't want to say it on the phone."

For a brief moment Emma felt relieved, but then Alice continued. "So I went into a shop, bought a writing pad and some envelopes and I wrote him another letter. I went through everything I'd said in the first letter and told my dad exactly why I'd said it. And I said I was wrong to write such an angry letter but it was only because he found it so difficult to talk to me. It took ages to write, but it was worth it."

Emma had one, last hope. "But you haven't posted it? Not yet?"

"Yeah, I posted it on the way back."

"Oh, Alice," said Emma.

"What's wrong? You said I shouldn't have written the first letter. You didn't want to post it."

"No," said Emma, reaching into her coat pocket, "I didn't want to post the first letter." She took out the original letter. "And I didn't."

Alice stared in horror at the envelope then snatched it from Emma's hands.

"But why?" she gasped. "You told me you posted it."

"I couldn't."

"But I asked you again this morning. You said you posted it."

"I thought you wanted me to say that. I didn't know what to do."

"Oh, Emma, how could you do this to me?"

Nikki had been listening without interrupting, but this was too much. "How could she do it you!" she said angrily. "How could you do what you've been doing to her?"

"What's it got to do with you?" shouted Alice. "Keep out of this. I didn't ask you to come here."

"Emma asked me to come. I wanted to help her. She's my friend."

"I thought she was my friend, too."

"I am your friend," shouted Emma.

"Oh yeah, a real friend, look what…"

Before Alice could finish there was a thunderous sound of footsteps on the stairs and Emma's mum burst into the room.

"What's going on?" she roared. She saw her daughter in tears on the bed and turned furiously to Alice.

"That's it!" she said. "That's enough. I'm speaking to your dad tonight. I'm not having you coming here and ruining Emma's holiday, and everyone else's as well."

Alice tried to speak. "But…"

"I don't want to hear about it, Alice. We've tried to help. All of us. But you just don't want to be helped."

"But I do. I…"

"Go downstairs, Emma," said Emma's mum before Alice could finish. "And you too, Nikki. I'm sorry you had to hear this."

Emma tried to speak in Alice's defence. "Mum…"

"Just go downstairs. Now!"

Emma got up from her bed and went out of the room with Nikki. Emma's mum turned back to her niece. "I'm going out," she said. "I've got to meet your uncle from work. When I get back I'll phone your dad and we'll sort this out once and for all. I suggest you stay up here until then."

The door slammed shut as she went out of the room.

Emma and Nikki were sitting silently in the kitchen when Emma's mum came in.

"I'm going to pick your dad up," she said before Emma could speak. "Just leave her alone until we get back. Let her calm down." And with that, she went out.

But Alice couldn't calm down. She sat in Emma's bedroom and sobbed. Everyone had turned against her. Her cousin, her cousin's friends and now even her aunt. Everything had gone wrong and even when she tried to put it right she just made it worse.

The letter to her dad was still in her hands. She began to tear it, first in half and then into smaller and smaller pieces. She stood up and dropped the pieces into the wastebasket by the side of Emma's dressing table. Then she went to the wardrobe and opened the doors.

Nikki and Emma were still sitting at the kitchen table.

"Didn't do much good, did I?" said Nikki.

"You didn't get a chance," replied Emma.

Nikki sighed. "She can't help a lot of what she's doing. She doesn't mean to do it, it just happens. I know, I remember."

"But you're alright now."

"Yeah, but it took a long time. All this has just happened to Alice. Maybe she needs help, like I did. Counselling. I wish she'd let me talk to her."

Before Emma could answer they heard footsteps coming down the stairs. The door opened and Alice came in. She was wearing her coat and carrying her suitcase.

"Alice, what are you doing?" asked Emma.

"It's obvious that no-one wants me here, so I'm going home," said Alice, walking towards the back door.

"But you can't," said Emma. "You can't just go."

"Can't I?" said Alice, pausing by the door. "I'm going home. To my real home. You'd better tell your mum and dad I'm catching the train. If they're interested."

"But Alice…"

"Don't worry, I'll be alright."

She opened the door and went out.

Emma went to get up. "I'll have to stop her…"

"No, let me go," said Nikki. "Stay here."

Nikki jumped up and ran out. She spotted Alice walking towards the town, but slowly. The suitcase was heavy and Alice was constantly switching it from one hand to the other. Nikki quickly caught her up.

"Can I talk to you?" she said. "Please?"

"Do what you like," said Alice, stopping to switch the case again. "It won't make any difference, I'm still going." She started walking again.

"I know how you're feeling," said Nikki.

"Do you?" Alice replied. "I doubt it."

"It's like nobody understands you," said Nikki. "Nobody really listens to how you're feeling. Nobody talks to you. Or explains. When you need them to. Isn't it?"

Alice stopped, put down the case and picked it up with the other hand. She began walking again. "Something like that," she said.

"My parents split up when I was four," said Nikki. "I lived with my mum and Greg stayed with Dad. My mum got married again. I thought her new husband was alright, at first. Then he started…"

Alice was walking more slowly, listening closely to what Nikki was saying.

"He what?"

"He started beating me up."

Alice stopped. She turned and looked at Nikki. "I didn't know."

Nikki shrugged. "Why should you?" she said. "It's not something I talk about very much."

Alice let the suitcase rest on the ground. "What happened?"

"It's alright now. They sent him to prison."

"I'm sorry," said Alice softly.

Nikki smiled. "That's not why I told you."

"Why, then?" asked Alice.

"I just wanted you to stop walking," said Nikki with a smile.

Alice returned the smile.

"I came to live with my dad," said Nikki. "Everyone tried to be nice to me. To protect me. My dad, my step-mum, Maggie, even my real mum when it came to it, in court. But I didn't want them to be nice, I wanted them to be real."

Alice nodded and Nikki continued. "I didn't want to be treated like a kid. I didn't want them to go around pretending it hadn't happened, or that they couldn't mention it because it might upset me. That's what upset me, playing happy families, pretending everything was normal when it wasn't."

Nikki paused. "They think we can't take the truth, don't they?" she added.

Alice nodded. "What's it like now?"

"It's better," said Nikki. "It's not perfect, but it's better. Maggie's good, she understands."

"My dad won't talk and my mum... she can't, not about how I'm feeling anyway," said Alice.

"What about your dad's girlfriend?" said Nikki.

"I don't know. I don't really know her."

"Maybe you should try to get to know her."

Alice looked at the suitcase standing on the pavement.

"You can't run away from it, Alice," said Nikki. "I tried but it doesn't work. You have to face up to it."

Nikki reached down and picked up Alice's suitcase. "Come back with me, Alice," she said.

Alice looked back down the road to Emma's house, and then at Nikki.

YOU CHOOSE DOES ALICE GO BACK?

YES GO TO PAGE 134

NO GO TO PAGE 120

There was no-one there. But Alice had heard the floorboard creak and she was certain she had heard a footstep. But there was no-one there. It's just the building, she thought. It must have been. Old buildings sometimes make strange noises. That must have been it. That's all it was.

She was so nervous she could hear her own breathing. She glanced back at the DJ deck. The posters were completely out of sight. It could be days before anyone found them. Or weeks. Or even months. She walked, as softly as possible, out of the room, stood at the top of the stairs and peered cautiously over the handrail. There was no-one to be seen. The Grove was silent.

Alice stepped on to the old staircase. The stairs creaked and groaned at almost every step, and all the way down Alice feared that one of the Grovers would walk out of a room and question her. But no-one did. She reached the ground floor and hurried out of the building.

As soon as Ben heard Alice making her way down the stairs he crept out from the tiny storeroom opposite the attic. Ben had followed Alice carefully, silently, and watched, almost in disbelief, as she pushed the last of the posters into the gap between the DJ deck and the wall. Then he trod on a loose floorboard. He saw Alice freeze, and in the brief moments she took to stand and look back, Ben slipped noiselessly into the storeroom.

He wasn't sure why. He just knew he wanted to help Alice. And as he waited, hardly daring to breath, he decided he had to retrieve the posters and put them back on the walls. There might just be time. If he was quick. He would talk to Alice afterwards. He would make her realise how stupid and reckless she had been.

He heard Alice walk on to the landing and stop. For a moment he feared she would turn back and look into the storeroom and see him hiding. But she didn't, she just hurried down the stairs.

Ben ran into the attic room, kneeled by the DJ deck and began pulling out the posters. It was difficult, some of the posters had slipped out of reach. He pushed his arm into the gap but couldn't get to the last few. Ben stood up and hauled the heavy deck away from the wall. Precious seconds passed as he dragged it across the floor and let it crash against the opposite wall. Anyone in the room below would have heard the noise, but it was a chance he had to take.

He scooped up the remaining posters from the dusty floor, dashed out of the attic and bounded down the stairs, almost falling in his desperate flight to reach the ground floor. But he made it, and no-one had seen him. He hurtled along the corridor towards the general room, but just as he turned the corner, he heard voices. The Grovers, led by Regina, were coming back into the building.

Ben skidded to a halt but not quickly enough. The Grovers had seen him. They stopped. And stared. The jumble of posters was plainly visible in his arms.

"What are you doing? Why have you got the posters?" shouted Regina, glaring at Ben.

"Yeah, what's going on, Ben?" asked Karen. "What are you playing at?"

Ben didn't answer. He couldn't. He'd been caught. Red-handed.

"He's taken the posters," said Regina. "He's got the posters!"

Everyone could see that Ben had the posters. But he said nothing. He just looked, shame-faced, at his friends, and at Alice, who was standing at the back of the group.

Now Alice could hardly believe what she was seeing. She had run out of the building and joined the others in the grounds. No-one particularly noticed, or if they did, no-one particularly cared. Everyone was too busy listening to Regina. Except for Emma.

Emma had been worrying about her cousin and wondering where she was. Every few minutes she had glanced towards the doorway in the hope that Alice might emerge. She noticed Ben creep away and go into the building but thought nothing of it. He was probably just bored. Then a few minutes later she saw Alice hurrying across the grass towards them. Emma was glad. Perhaps it meant that, at last, Alice was trying to show an interest in what was going on at the Grove.

Now both Emma and Alice watched in horror as the Grovers slowly gathered around Ben. Emma was certain now that she had seen Ben slip away to snatch the posters. But she was wrong. Alice knew the truth. There had been someone watching her in the attic. She did hear a footstep. It was Ben. But why did he have the posters? What was he trying to do?

Ben was thinking, desperately searching for a way out of the mess he had landed himself in. He smiled. "I was just having a laugh," he said unconvincingly. "I was gonna hide them, for a while. I would have told you where they were. It was just a laugh. That's all."

But no-one was laughing, or even smiling, not even Ben's closest friends, Ollie and Liam.

"Look at the posters," snarled Regina. "They're all creased. I bet some of them are ruined."

"Yeah, well, sorry about that," said Ben. "It was an accident. I suppose it was a bit of a stupid thing to do, really. But it was only a joke."

Tina stepped forward and took the posters from Ben's hands. "Not much of a joke, was it Ben?" she said.

Ben shrugged. What could he say? He wouldn't split on Alice. His only chance now was if she confessed. He looked straight at Alice, their eyes met and Alice knew exactly what the look meant. He's waiting for me to tell them it was me, she thought. But I can't, I can't!

Ben could see the fear in Alice's eyes. He smiled, trying to reassure her that if she couldn't confess then he certainly wasn't going to say a word. But Alice looked away.

Ben shrugged his shoulders. There was no alternative. He had to go.

"Sorry," he mumbled softly, and he began edging his way through the crowd. The Grovers stepped aside to let him pass. Ben reached the front door and stepped into the open air.

"And don't come back," he heard Regina shout as he walked down the drive.

• • • • •

"I don't understand it," said Emma. "Why would Ben do a thing like that?"

Alice didn't answer. She was glad that Emma couldn't see her.

The two girls were in bed. It was late, but after the excitement at the Grove, Emma was finding it impossible to sleep. Alice was also wide awake and she was also thinking about Ben.

She couldn't forget the way he had looked at her. She realised now that Ben had been trying to help her by putting the posters back in the general room. But she also realised that when Ben looked at her she had failed to help him. She had let him down and she felt deeply ashamed.

"Alice?" called Emma softly.

"Yes?" Alice eventually replied.

"You didn't answer me?"

"What?"

"I asked you why you thought Ben had done it?"

"How should I know?" said Alice. "I hardly know him."
"But he likes you."
"So? That's not my fault, is it?"
"And I have seen you talking to him a couple of times."
"When?" said Alice, a little too loudly.
"Ssshh," said Emma. "You'll wake Mum and Dad."
"When did you see me with him?" said Alice in a loud whisper.
"I thought I saw you with him in the pool room."
"I was only there for a minute. That's all. I hardly spoke to him."
"Oh," said Emma. They were silent for a few moments. Emma was still trying to work out why Ben had acted in the way he had. "But what a stupid thing to do," she said. "Ben's not a kid, like Stumpy, or even Barry or Bradley. He's not usually stupid. And now he's been suspended from the Grove."

Alice shivered. It wasn't the cold. Ben was suspended from the Grove. Tina had made the decision soon after Ben walked out. He was suspended indefinitely, she told them. No-one protested. No-one argued. And no-one spoke up in Ben's defence.

Alice shifted in her bed and pulled the duvet up around her head.
"You didn't see him, did you?" asked Emma.
"Who?"
"Ben, of course."
"When?" said Alice anxiously.
"I saw him go inside, just before you came out. I thought you might have seen him."
"No, I didn't see him, and I didn't talk to him. I've told you." At least that much was true. Alice hadn't seen Ben and she hadn't spoken to him. Not at that time. But, unlike everyone else at Byker Grove, Alice knew exactly what Ben had been doing, and why.
"I just don't understand it," said Emma again.
"Look, you've said that," said Alice. "Can we go to sleep now, please? I'm tired. I don't want to talk anymore."

• • • • •

Ben was the talk of Byker Grove. In every room, in the grounds, wherever there were Grovers, the topic of conversation was the same – Ben Carter.

Claire, Nat and Teraise were in the games room.

"I don't see the point," said Claire "I mean, it wasn't funny. What was he getting at?"

"He just got himself thrown out," said Teraise. "Crazy if you ask me."

"Well, that is the point," said Nat. "Lads. They're all crazy when it comes down to it."

Bill and Stumpy, closely followed by Wombat, were scrambling over the climbing frame. "D'you think he did it because he wanted his poster to win?" shouted Stumpy.

"No," Bill shouted back. "He didn't even do a poster."

Nikki and Matt were just arriving at the Grove. They were walking through the gate separating Nikki's back garden from the Byker grounds when they heard the young boys shout.

"I feel a bit sorry for him," said Matt.

"Ben?" asked Nikki.

Matt nodded. "Probably didn't mean any harm."

"Yeah, but some of the posters were ruined."

"They weren't ruined, just a bit creased."

Some of the posters were a bit creased. And Regina wasn't very happy about it. She and Laura were busy fixing the posters back on to the general room walls. The judging of the poster competition was due to take place in less than an hour and Regina wanted all the posters back in their original positions before then.

"I don't see why they all have to be in the same place," said Laura, passing one of the crumpled posters to her friend.

"Because that's where they were before," said Regina. "That's where they all looked best. I want the judges to see them where they look best. I want it to be fair."

She fixed the poster to the wall and picked up another. "Look at this?" she snapped. "It's mine. Look how creased it is."

"It's not too bad," said Laura. "You can hardly notice. Where does it go?"

"Right in the middle of that wall," said Regina, pointing to her chosen space. "So the judges see it as they come through the door."

Laura smiled. "Oh, yes. We want it to be fair, don't we Regina?"

Regina ignored her friend and attempted to smooth out a tiny crease in her poster.

The poster competition judges were in the office with Tina.

"There must be something else," said Karen. "Something he didn't tell us."

"What?" said Cher.

"I don't know," said Karen with a shrug. "But I know Ben. There's something else."

"Well, we won't find out, will we?" said Sita. "Not with him suspended."

The three girls looked at Tina. "Well?" asked Karen.

"Well, what?" replied Tina.

"How long is he gonna be suspended?"

"I told you yesterday," said Tina firmly. "Indefinitely."

"Yeah, but how long is indefinitely?"

"I haven't decided yet. But I'll let you know when I have."

Liam and Ollie were playing pool. "He didn't say a thing last night," said Liam. "I asked him. Wouldn't say a word."

"I bet Lou's not very pleased," said Ollie.

"He hasn't told Lou," said Liam.

Greg was watching the game. "They'll have to let him come back. It was stupid but we've all done worse things."

In the general room Regina was fixing the final poster back in position. She stood back and admired all the posters. "How could he do it?" she said. "Everyone's worked so hard on them."

"He probably wasn't thinking about that," said Laura. "He just thought it was funny."

"Well, it wasn't," said Regina sharply, as Emma and Alice walked into the room.

"Hello," said Regina. She turned back to Laura. "I'm glad he's suspended and I hope Tina doesn't let him back. Ever."

"Regina, he'll have to come back at some time," said Laura.

"Not before my saving energy day," snapped Regina. "Or the party."

Emma joined Regina in the centre of the room and slowly turned in a complete circle so that she could look at all the posters.

"Do they look alright?" asked Regina. "Can you see the creases?"

Emma shook her head. "Hardly at all," she said. "They look great. Don't they Alice?"

But Alice didn't look at the posters. She couldn't bear to see them. Alice didn't want to be at the Grove or anywhere near it. She had tried to talk Emma into going into town to see a film or to go shopping. But Emma told her they had to be at the Grove for the judging of the poster competition. So they were there. But Alice couldn't look at the posters.

She found a chair in the conservatory and sat gazing out through the windows. She wanted to own up. She wanted to shout out: "It wasn't Ben, it was me." But she couldn't do it. She didn't have the nerve.

Regina ignored Alice. She had tried to help her the previous day. But Alice made it clear she didn't want Regina's help. She called her a stupid kid and told her to leave her alone. Well, Regina was leaving her alone. She was ignoring her.

Regina took a final admiring look at the posters. "All ready for the judging later on," she said to Laura. "Let's go and tell Tina."

Regina and Laura walked out into the corridor and Emma went through to the conservatory and sat next to Alice.

Emma was worried. Alice had been moody and unhappy all week. They had argued and Emma was thoroughly fed up with her cousin. But today was different. Alice was more than moody, more than unhappy. She was nervous. And frightened.

"Alice," Emma said gently, "is there something wrong?"

"Of course there's something wrong," said Alice irritably. "My mum and dad have split up."

"I know that, Alice," said Emma patiently, "but is there something else?"

"What d'you mean, something else? What else could there be?"

"I don't know. Something. Is it Ben?"

"Why d'you keep asking me about Ben?" snapped Alice.

Emma could see that Alice was growing angry. But she was certain there was something her cousin wasn't telling her. So she persisted. "I just thought he might have said something to you."

"I told you he didn't say anything."

"But yesterday, are you sure you didn't see him? Before you came out?"

"I didn't see him," said Alice, glaring at her cousin. "I told you last night that I didn't see him. Why d'you keep asking me? I didn't see him, I wasn't in here and it's got nothing to do with me!"

"I didn't say it had something to do with…"

"Well, leave it then!" shouted Alice.

The conversation was on the verge of erupting into another

furious row, but Emma was determined not to argue again with her cousin. "Alright," she said softly. "I was only trying to help."

Alice stood up. "Just leave it, Emma," she said. "You can't help. No-one can help." She turned away and walked back through the general room and out into the corridor.

Emma sighed as she watched Alice go. She did want to help. There was something wrong. Something more. And it did have something to do with Ben. She just knew it. And she couldn't just let Alice walk away again. She got up to follow her.

Tina was standing by the office door talking to Regina and Laura.

"Did you see where my cousin went?" asked Emma.

"Outside," said Tina. "She didn't look very happy."

"She never looks very happy," said Regina as Emma hurried out through the front door.

There was no sign of Alice. Emma wandered over to the treehouse where Stumpy sat talking to Bill. Wombat was scratching and sniffing around in the dirt. He looked up as Emma approached and trotted towards her.

"Have you seen my cousin?" asked Emma, glancing up to where the two boys sat.

"She went down the drive," said Stumpy. "She just ignored Wombat. He only wanted to be stroked."

Emma smiled down at Stumpy's dog. "Well, I won't ignore you, will I, Wombat?" she said, reaching out to tickle him behind the ears.

"He likes that," said Stumpy.

"I know he does," said Emma. "But I've got to find Alice. Now."

She gave Wombat one last vigorous scratch and then started off down the drive. Wombat went to follow her.

"Wombat!" called Stumpy. Wombat stopped and looked back at his master. "Here!" called Stumpy. Wombat sniffed and looked away. "Here!" called Stumpy, a little more loudly. Wombat scratched behind his ear in exactly the same place as Emma had and then reluctantly padded back to the base of the tree. He sniffed the dirt, chased his tail in two full circles and then lay down. "Good boy," said Stumpy.

Emma walked quickly down the sloping drive and turned in the direction of her home. She saw Alice immediately. But she wasn't alone. There was a bus shelter about fifty metres away on the opposite side of the road. Alice was there. And so was Ben.

Emma stopped. Ben. She knew it. She stepped back into the drive so that she couldn't be seen. They were too far away for Emma to hear what was being said, but she could see that Ben was doing most of the talking. Alice was staring down at the ground, hardly speaking at all. The one-way conversation went on for several minutes until finally Ben shook his head and walked away, without looking back.

Emma quickly crossed the road, and ran to the bus shelter. Alice was slumped on the seat. She didn't even hear Emma approach.

"Alice, please tell me what's going on," said Emma.

Alice didn't answer. Emma sat down next to her cousin.

"Why was Ben here, Alice? What did he want?"

"He was waiting for me."

"But why? Did you know he'd be here?"

"He wanted to talk. He said he thought I'd turn up if he waited long enough. He thought I'd be with you."

"But what did he want?"

Alice shook her head.

"It was about yesterday, wasn't it?" said Emma. "When he took the posters?"

Alice looked up slowly and gazed into the distance.

"Alice, what is it? Tell me."

"Can't you guess?" Alice whispered.

"I don't want to guess, I want you to tell me…" Emma stopped. She stared at her cousin. Her face was pale. Frightened. Terrified. And then Emma knew the truth. "It wasn't Ben," she said slowly. "He didn't take the posters, did he? It was you!"

Alice couldn't look at her cousin. "I hid them in the attic," she said, so quietly that Emma could hardly hear the words.

"Why?" said Emma. "Why did you do it?"

"I don't know why," said Alice tearfully. "I was angry. Everyone kept telling me what to do and how I should be. You. Regina. Even Ben. I took the posters and I hid them in the attic. Ben saw me and followed me. I didn't know. I didn't know until we came in and saw him standing there with the posters in his hands." She turned towards her cousin at last. "He wasn't taking the posters, Emma, he was putting them back. He was trying to help me."

Emma stood up. "And you let him take the blame," she said angrily. "When he was trying to save you. You let him take the blame and get himself thrown out of the Grove."

"I wanted to say something, but I couldn't, I just couldn't." Alice leaned forward and put her head in her hands.

"Oh, don't start crying again," said Emma furiously. "I'm not feeling sorry for you anymore. I can't believe you've done this. It's terrible. Horrible."

Alice looked up at her. "Ben said if I went back and told them what really happened, and apologised, they might forgive me and give me another chance."

"And are you going to?" asked her cousin bitterly.

"I don't know if I can. Ben won't split on me. He said it's up to me."

Emma had always liked her cousin. The past week had been difficult but Emma had not stopped liking Alice. Until now. At that moment she didn't like Alice one bit. She despised her.

"Ben won't split on you," she said quietly, "but I will." She didn't give Alice the opportunity to reply. "I will, Alice," she continued. "Unless you come back with me now and tell them the truth."

"But..."

"Now," said Emma. She turned away and strode off towards the Grove. Alice stood up and followed her.

• • • • •

Nearly all the Grovers had arrived for the judging of the poster competition. They waited – impatiently – in the pool room, in the games room, on the stairs and around the office. Only Sita, Cher and Karen were in the general room. They were reaching their decision. The winning poster was being selected.

Regina sat on the stairs, talking to anyone who would listen. "I've done my best but some of them are ruined, including mine."

"They're not ruined," said Nikki, remembering what Matt had said earlier. "Just a bit creased."

"Yeah, but they won't choose a poster that's creased or lined, will they? It's just not fair."

"You've got as much chance as anyone else," said Nikki. "They won't worry about a few creases."

Emma and Alice walked through the main entrance just as Karen stepped into the corridor. "If you'd all like to come in, we're ready to announce our decision."

Emma glared at Alice. "After they've told us who's won," she said, making sure that no-one else could hear. "Do it then. And make sure you do, or I will."

The general room filled quickly as Grovers appeared from all over the building. Everyone was anxious to learn the identity of the winner. Everyone wanted to know whose poster would be going off to be printed and distributed around the town. They filed into the room and sat on chairs and tables. Sita, Cher and Karen were waiting on the stage.

"Right," said Karen. "It's been a very difficult decision and we were really impressed with the standard of the entries."

"Oh, get on with it," said Ollie. "Who's won?"

"We're trying to tell you," answered Sita.

"Shut up, Ollie," said Liam.

Sita continued. "As you know, it was decided that the judges wouldn't know the identity of the artists. That's why all the posters have a number next to them."

"Yeah, yeah," said Ollie. "We know."

"You could have had a look when you were in here on your own," said Bradley. "How do we know someone hasn't paid you to pick their poster?"

"Because we're honest," said Cher. "Do you want to know who's won or not?"

"Yes!" came the shout from several voices.

"Alright then," said Cher. "The winner is…" She looked at Karen and Sita. They had decided that all three of them would announce the winning number at the same time.

"Poster number… fourteen," they said together.

Everyone in the room, even Alice, scanned the walls until every eye rested on the winning poster. Alice gasped. The huge, smiling, bright yellow face grinned out at her. The bright blue eyes seemed to be staring straight at her. Underneath the face, in shimmering red letters, the message read: 'Be Happy – Save Energy.' It was that poster. The one she hated so much. The first one she had ripped from the wall.

"Whose is it?" said Regina. "Who did it?"

A loud yell came from close to the stage. "Yes!" cried Bradley. "Yes!" He threw both arms up into the air and began marching victoriously around the room. "Champion! Champion!" he shouted.

Ollie laughed. "Still reckon it was a fix, do you, Bradley?"
"How much did you pay them, then?" called Liam.
"It's no fix," said Bradley, leaping on to the stage and punching the air in triumph. "They just knew a fantastic piece of art when they saw it. Just wait till it's all over the town. I'll be famous."
Bradley was enjoying his moment of glory. "I want to say thanks to the judges," he shouted, "and to everyone else who had a go. I'm sure you all agree with me that the best man won."
"Told you they wouldn't pick mine," said Regina to Laura.
Barry was close enough to hear Regina's comment. "Yeah, but yours was terrible anyway," he said.
Bradley called to Regina from the stage. "Better get my poster down to the printers straight away, Regina. I'll come with you, if you like. Make sure it gets there OK. We don't want anything else to go wrong, do we?"
"Don't worry, Bradley," called Tina from the doorway. "I'll make sure your poster gets to the printers."
She turned to go back to the office and some of the Grovers also began to drift away. Emma glared at her cousin and indicated to her urgently that now was the moment for her to step on to the stage and own up. But Alice didn't move. She stared, her eyes wide with fear, back at her cousin.
"Come on," mouthed Emma. Still Alice didn't move. She just shook her head slightly.
"Right," said Emma. She strode across the room, climbed on to the stage and brushed the still celebrating Bradley aside.
"Careful," he said. "What d'you want? I won, not you."
Emma ignored Bradley. "Just a minute, everyone," she shouted loudly. "There's something I've got to say."
The Grovers stopped and glanced back at the stage in surprise. Emma didn't usually make speeches or announcements at Byker Grove. She was one of the quiet Grovers. She usually left public speaking to people like Regina. But even Tina had heard Emma shout. She walked back to hear what Emma had to say and stood at the back of the huddle of Grovers blocking the doorway.
The room went quiet as Emma turned to her cousin again. Alice wanted to run out. But she couldn't move. She gazed back at Emma. Surely she wouldn't really do it. Surely she wouldn't really split on her own cousin.

The seconds ticked by. Still Emma waited. Still Alice didn't move.

"Well?" called Regina. "Come on, Emma, what is it you want to say?"

"Alright," said Emma. She took a deep breath and one final look in her cousin's direction.

YOU CHOOSE DOES EMMA SPLIT ON ALICE?

YES GO TO THE NEXT PAGE

NO GO TO PAGE 147

Alice was staring at the floor. Everyone else was staring at Emma. She felt herself tremble. She was nervous. Her mouth was dry and the palms of her hands were moist and clammy.

"I didn't want to say this," said Emma softly.

"Speak up," shouted Ollie from the doorway. "If you've got something to say, let's hear it."

"Ssshh." said Tina. "Give her a chance."

Emma coughed and cleared her throat.

"Come on, Emma love," called Tina. "We're all listening."

"It's about Ben," said Emma much more loudly.

The Grovers groaned. Ben was old news. He was suspended and that was that. The Grovers were expecting to hear something new. Something interesting. The group in the doorway turned to file out and other Grovers went to follow them.

"He didn't do it!"

Everyone froze. Everyone heard those four short words. They seemed to echo around the room. The Grovers stared at Emma. They were silent. No-one muttered, or laughed, or shuffled their feet. The room was absolutely quiet.

Emma swallowed and continued. "Ben wasn't taking the posters away when we saw him yesterday, he was trying to put them back."

Emma could see puzzled and confused looks on the faces of many of the Grovers. "Ben saw someone else take the posters," she said quickly. "He saw someone else take them up to the attic and hide them and then run away. Ben was trying to save her. He was going to put the posters back on the walls as though nothing had happened."

Emma paused.

"It was her," murmured Ollie to Liam. "She did it. She's owning up to save Ben."

Tina was just standing behind them. "I don't think so," she whispered, glancing towards Alice.

"Was it you?" shouted Ollie at Emma. "Did you take them?"

"No," answered Emma. "It wasn't me."

"Then who was it?" said Regina. "Come on Emma, you've got to tell us."

"It was…" Emma looked across at Alice, who slowly lifted her head. "It was my cousin," said Emma. "It was Alice."

Every Grover looked at Alice, their faces hostile, their eyes glaring.

Tina quickly pushed her way through the group of Grovers in the doorway and went up to Alice. "Is it true?" she said quietly, already certain that Emma had spoken the truth.

Alice nodded.

"Well, what have you got to say about it?"

"I... I..." But Alice couldn't continue. She shook her head slightly and rushed out of the room, her face burning under the accusing looks of the Grovers. Emma jumped from the stage and ran after her.

• • • • •

There was a knock at the front door but Ben didn't move. He was at home, watching television. He didn't particularly want to watch television but he had nothing else to do. All his friends were at the Grove and Ben couldn't go to the Grove.

There was a second knock, louder this time. Ben still didn't move. He just reached for the television remote control and turned up the volume.

Ben's foster mother, Lou, poked her head around the door. "Don't you trouble yourself, Ben," she said. "I'll get it. I've got nothing better to do. I don't think."

"It won't be for me, anyway," said Ben quietly, as Lou stomped away towards the front door. "No-one wants to speak to me."

But Ben was wrong. Lou reappeared a few minutes later. "There's someone to see you," she said, shaking her head. "Why didn't you tell them the truth, Ben? You daft thing."

Lou looked back into the hallway. "Come in, love," she said. She stepped aside and Tina entered the room.

"Oh," said Ben. "You know, then?"

Tina nodded. "We know."

"You better sit down, Tina," said Lou, "and I'll leave you to it."

"No, don't go, Lou," said Ben, standing up and switching off the television. "I should have told you about this last night, but... you know."

"Yeah, I know," said Lou with a rueful smile. "Well, we'd best all sit down then, hadn't we? I wondered why you were hanging around watching the telly."

Lou was the person Ben admired and respected most. He had been through difficult and painful times. He had been abandoned by his dad, rejected by his grandfather and then deserted by his older brother. But ever since Ben had come to live at Gallagher's, through all the difficulties, and even when he had been close to serious trouble with the police, Lou had stuck by Ben. Lou cared about Ben, and Ben cared about Lou.

"Well, come on then, let's hear it," said Lou, and she and Tina settled into their chairs and waited for Ben to speak.

"I'm sorry," he said eventually.

"You could have told me the truth," said Tina. "You know you could. Even if you didn't want to say it in front of the others. I had to suspend you. I had no option."

"Suspended is he?" asked Lou, her faced concerned.

"Not anymore."

"Oh, well that's something, at least."

"It was very noble of you, Ben," said Tina.

"Noble? What's that supposed to mean?"

"Taking the blame. Protecting Alice like that."

"Yeah, well, I know what it's like, don't I? Parents messing your life up. And anyway, it was partly my fault that she did it."

"Your fault? How was it your fault?"

"She came into the pool room just before she took the posters. I was trying to impress her. I said I knew all about her parents splitting up and that we could talk about it."

"So what's wrong with that?"

"I didn't know until today that everyone else had been doing the same thing. Telling her what to do. Giving her advice."

"Yeah, but they were only trying to help."

"But she doesn't want our help. She wants her mum and dad to talk to her. But they won't, or they can't."

"You've seen her today, then, Ben?" asked Lou.

"I waited for her outside the Grove." He turned to Tina. "She didn't really want to ruin those posters, Tina. She's just angry. I was angry when it happened to me. With my dad and my grandad and even Terry. I did some stupid things. If people treat you like a little kid, you start acting like a little kid."

Lou and Tina looked at each other. "I've never had half as much trouble with my kids as I have with their parents," said Lou with a sigh.

Tina nodded. "Poor girl. I wish I'd known all this before." She smiled at Ben. "You will come back tomorrow, won't you?"

"Are you sure Regina's forgiven me?" asked Ben with a grin.

"There's nothing to forgive. And anyway, you're quite the hero at the Grove now."

"Hero?"

"Standing up for your girlfriend like that."

"She's not my girlfriend."

"But you wouldn't mind if she was."

"She's got too much else on her mind."

Tina stood up to go. "Yeah, I reckon she has. But I hope she realises what a good friend she's got in you. I'll see you tomorrow. Bye, then, Lou."

"I'll see you out, love," said Lou, rising slowly from her chair.

"Tina?" said Ben.

Tina stopped at the door. "Yeah?"

"How did it go? When she came back? I told her that if she went back and apologised they might give her another chance."

"Oh, Ben," said Tina, "I'm sorry, you don't know, do you?"

"Don't know what?"

"Alice didn't apologise."

"What?"

"No. It wasn't Alice. Emma told us what really happened."

"But how did Emma know?"

"I don't know. She told us after the poster competition was judged. I could see she was waiting for Alice to speak up, but Alice wouldn't say a word. So Emma told us. She didn't want to, I could see that, too. I felt as sorry for Emma as I did for Alice."

"But can't you just forget it now?" asked Ben hopefully. "At least you know the truth. Can't you just leave it at that?"

Tina shook her head. "No, Ben, I can't. The other kids are furious. I couldn't suspend you and then do nothing when I learned the truth. If only she'd apologised or at least tried to explain. But she didn't, she just walked out. I had to ban her from the Grove, Ben. I had to."

• • • • •

"I don't know why you wanted to come here," said Alice.

"We had to go somewhere," Emma replied. "You wouldn't go home and you didn't want to go anywhere where we might see my friends. This was all I could think of."

They were sitting in a restaurant, but it wasn't the sort of restaurant either of them would usually have visited.

It was a huge, self-service cafe at the top of a department store in the city centre. They were surrounded by shoppers. Everyone seemed to be hurrying their way through plates of sandwiches or cakes and cups of tea or coffee.

Everyone but Alice and Emma. Their glasses were empty. They had been sitting at the table for some time.

"We can't stay for much longer," said Emma. "They'll be closing soon."

"You don't have to stay at all, if you don't want to," said Alice.

"Alice…"

"Don't try and make it all alright now, Emma," said Alice. "You split on me."

"I had to."

"Did you?"

"It wasn't fair on Ben."

Alice didn't answer immediately. "I'll never be able to go back to the Grove."

"Maybe you could. If you apologised."

Alice laughed. "And you think they'd listen?"

"I could talk to them first. Tell them you're really sorry."

"It's too late for being sorry."

Emma gazed around the busy restaurant. She had been there once before, with her mum, when they were searching for what her mum called 'sensible' shoes for school. She hadn't enjoyed being there then and she wasn't enjoying it now. She wanted to go home.

It had been a terrible day. After those few dreadful minutes in the general room she had run from the Grove expecting Alice to shout at her, or scream, or call her names. But she didn't. She said nothing. Not a word. She just walked to the bus stop where Emma had learned the truth about the posters and got on to the first bus that arrived. Emma got on too, and the bus carried them into the city.

Alice wouldn't talk, except to say that she didn't want to go home and she didn't want to see any of Emma's friends. So they trailed around the city centre until finally Emma suggested they went into the department store. They were still there, staring at empty glasses.

"I'll have to pretend I'm going to the Grove every day," said Alice suddenly.

"What?"

"That's what I'll do. I'm not going home. I can't let my mum or dad know what's happened, so I'll have to pretend. It's only another week."

"But you can't!"

"I can, and I will," said Alice, glaring at her cousin. "Don't tell your mum, Emma. You've split on me once, don't do it again." Alice pushed her chair away from the table. "Come on, let's go," she said.

They rode back on the bus. As it stopped and started it's way through the rush-hour traffic Alice gazed through the window and thought about her dad. He would be driving home too. It was Friday evening, the beginning of the weekend. But Alice's dad wouldn't be driving back to their home, the home he had shared with Alice and her mum, he was returning to his home. With Cheryl.

Alice felt like crying. She used to love weekends, specially Sundays. Her parents were busy with their jobs during the week, and often on Saturdays too, but Sundays always used to be their day, the day they spent together. Alice and her dad were great friends, best friends, he used to say when she was younger.

But that was before. Now his best friend was Cheryl and Alice dreaded weekends. Their tiny flat was too small for them all to sit around in so Alice and her dad usually went out. Visiting her grandparents, sitting in burger bars or going swimming because there was nothing else to do. But it wasn't the same without her mum there too, it wasn't special anymore.

It often seemed to Alice as though her dad was counting off the minutes until he could take her home and go back to Cheryl. She knew her dad had stopped loving her mum, but sometimes it seemed to Alice as though he had stopped loving her as well.

She knew that both her mum and dad would be terribly hurt and disappointed if they discovered what had happened at the Grove. But Alice was hurt and disappointed. By them, specially her dad. It was all his fault. He had left them and he didn't understand the way Alice felt. He didn't even try to understand.

The bus was hot and stuffy. Alice was tired. Exhausted. She felt her eyes beginning to close and slowly her head slid to one side until it rested on Emma's shoulder.

Emma looked down at her unhappy cousin. "Oh, Alice," she whispered.

• • • • •

"Welcome back, lover boy," said Karen with a grin.

"My hero," squealed Cher, fluttering her eyelashes and pretending to swoon.

"Oh, he's dead romantic, and dead dishy," added Sita, as she gazed dreamy-eyed at the object of their amusement. "I wish someone would sacrifice themselves like that for me."

Ben stood, hands on hips, waiting for the dramatic presentation to end.

The three girls smiled false smiles and sighed in unison.

"Have you finished?" said Ben.

"We've only just started," said Karen. "You'll never live this down." She clasped her hands together and gazed upwards. "Ben Carter, the boy who was thrown out of the Grove to save the honour of his true love," she said wistfully.

"Oh, come on, give it a rest," said Ben.

Ben was back at the Grove and he was glad to be back. But he hadn't expected a reception quite like this. The three girls stood aside and sighed again as he walked by.

He heard their laughter as he went into the general room where Regina and her gang were seated at a table.

Regina glanced up. "Oh, it's you," she said. "That was a pretty stupid thing to do, wasn't it? Wasting everyone's time like that."

"That's more like it," said Ben with a laugh.

"More like what?" asked Regina with a puzzled expression on her face.

"More like I was expecting. Thanks very much, Regina."

Regina gazed at her friends as Ben left the room. "What's he talking about?" she said.

No-one replied. They were anxious for Regina to get on with the meeting she had called, or rather, they were anxious for the meeting to be over so that they could get on with what they wanted to do.

"Why did he thank me?" said Regina, still wondering about Ben.

"Oh, come on, Regina," said Barry. "Can we get on?"

Regina dismissed Ben from her thoughts. "We're having this meeting so that we can decide on the rules and regulations for my *Don't Waste Energy Day*."

"You mean our *Don't Waste Energy Day*, don't you?" said Laura.

"What do we need rules for?" asked Stumpy. "Haven't we got enough rules already?"

"We've got to have rules. That way everyone knows exactly what they can and can't do," said Regina firmly. "I'm going to write them out and put them on the noticeboard."

She picked up her pen and prepared to write. "Rule number one is that no more than one light should be turned on in any room, and all lights should be switched off if there's no-one in the room."

"Is that rule number two?" asked Barry.

"What?" said Regina.

"The bit about the lights being switched off if there's no-one in the room."

Regina scowled. "It doesn't matter if it's one rule or two rules, Barry. Let's just make up the rules, shall we?"

Bradley had been thinking. "Yeah, but if we switch all the lights off we won't be able to see the rules to read them, will we?" he said.

"Bradley!" Regina glared at Bradley. "Will you stop interrupting and let me get on? There's a lot to do."

Stumpy sighed. It looked as though it was going to be a long meeting.

Ben had made his way to the pool room where Ollie and Greg were delighted to see him.

"Well, I wouldn't have done it," Ollie told Ben. "Not for a girl. I might have done it for a mate, but not for a girl."

"Didn't do any good, anyway," added Greg. "She's banned and I can't see them letting her come back. Might as well forget about her, Ben."

Ben didn't reply. The trouble was, he didn't want to forget about her.

"Ben?"

Ben turned around. Emma was standing in the doorway.

"Can I talk to you for a minute?"

"Yeah," said Ben. "Yeah, alright."

He got up and followed Emma into the corridor.

"Shall we go outside?" said Emma. "I don't really want anyone else to hear."

They went out into the garden. It was cold and blustery so they found a bench close to the walls of the building.

"Where is she?" asked Ben as soon as he sat down.

"Gone into town," Emma replied.

"I thought she might have gone home."

"No, she hasn't gone home, that's the problem."

"Problem? What d'you mean?"

Emma told Ben everything that had happened since she and Alice had left the Grove, and about the secret that Alice had asked her to keep.

"And will you do it?" asked Ben when Emma had finished speaking.

"I have so far," said Emma. "I didn't tell my mum last night. But I hate lying to her."

"And she thinks Alice is here with you now?"

Emma nodded. "But I can't keep lying, I just can't. My mum'll see through it, anyway. What do I do, Ben?"

Ben shook his head. "I'm sorry, Emma," he said, "I don't know. Maybe you should…"

They heard footsteps and looked up to see Nikki approaching.

"Hi, Emma," she said.

Emma smiled.

"I'm glad you're back, Ben," Nikki continued. "I think it was really good of you to try and help Alice."

"Didn't help much, though, did it?" said Ben.

Nikki turned to Emma. "Are you alright?"

"Yeah, I suppose so," answered Emma.

"Where's Alice?"

"It's a long story," said Emma with a sigh.

"Do you want to tell me about it?"

Emma looked at Ben.

"Yeah," he said. "I think you should. She might be more help than me."

"You'd better sit down," said Emma to Nikki.

Nikki sat on the bench and listened in silence as Emma told the whole story for a second time.

Nikki sighed when Emma had finished. "Look, you know you asked me before if I'd talk to Alice?"

Emma nodded.

"Well, I wasn't sure. But I will, if you still want me to."

Ben thought back to his conversation with Tina and Lou the previous afternoon. "Yeah, but hasn't she had enough of all of us giving her advice about her parents?"

"I'm not gonna give her advice about her parents, Ben," said Nikki. "I'm the last one to give advice after the mess I've been in."

"What, then?" asked Ben.

"I just want to tell her that not everyone at the Grove is against her and that if she comes back some of us will be on her side." She turned to Emma. "What d'you think?"

"I think it's worth a try," said Emma.

"Let's go, then."

"D'you want me to come?" asked Ben.

"Maybe not, eh, Ben?" said Nikki. "She probably feels bad about what's happened to you. But we'll need your help when she comes back."

Ben nodded. "If she comes back."

Ben watched Emma and Nikki walk down the drive and then went back into the Grove. Bradley stood in the main corridor, talking excitedly to Karen, Sita and Cher.

"And I've decided that for the party I'm gonna do a famous old magic trick," he said.

"So," said Karen, "what's that got to do with us?"

"It needs a very glamorous female assistant."

"Oh yeah," said Cher. "And what is this trick, then?"

"It's called 'Sawing The Lady In Half' and it'll be brilliant."

Karen, Sita and Cher turned and walked away without another word.

"No-one wants to do it," said Bradley. "What's wrong with the girls in this place?"

• • • • •

Emma and Nikki waited at the bus stop where Emma and Alice had arranged to meet. They were early and the minutes passed slowly. Eventually a bus appeared in the distance. It trundled slowly towards them and finally came to a standstill. The automatic doors hissed and folded back and an elderly lady carefully stepped off. But no-one else.

"D'you want this bus, or are you just bus spotting?" called the driver to Emma and Nikki. Emma shook her head. The doors closed and the bus moved noisily away leaving a cloud of smelly diesel fumes.

"She said she'd be on that one," said Emma to Nikki.

"I don't mind waiting," Nikki replied.

"I do," said Emma. They sat in the bus shelter and waited.

"If she's not on the next one I'm going home," said Emma irritably. "I'm fed up with running around after Alice."

But Alice was on the next bus. She looked miserable as she stepped down on to the pavement.

"You're late," said Emma, expecting an explanation from Alice. She didn't get one. Alice simply shrugged and glanced towards Nikki. "I didn't expect to see anyone from the Grove."

"I thought we could have a talk," said Nikki.

"What about?" said Alice. "I don't need any more advice, thank you very much. From anyone."

"Let's wait till we get home, shall we?" said Emma "Mum won't be back yet."

Emma and Nikki hardly spoke on the way to the house. They listened as Alice moaned on about how bored she'd been all day and how she hadn't spoken to a single person since she'd left the house that morning. Both Emma and Nikki felt like reminding Alice that she had no-one to blame for that but herself. But they didn't. They just listened. Very patiently.

"Well?" said Alice, when they had made their way up to Emma's bedroom and were sitting on the beds. "I suppose everyone's been talking about me all day. How awful I am. How terrible?"

"A lot of them, yeah," said Emma.

"But not everyone," said Nikki. "Look, Alice, you've got to come back to the Grove. You've got to apologise and try to put things right. You can't spend a whole week pretending to Emma's mum and dad. You'll get found out and then it'll be worse."

"They won't find out," snapped Alice. "Not unless Emma tells them. She's good at splitting on people."

"That's not very fair, Alice," said Nikki.

Alice looked at her cousin. "I know it's not," she said softly. "I'm sorry, Emma. I don't mean it. I don't blame you for telling them at the Grove. Not really. I thought you were brave to do it. Much braver than I am. It's just that… I keep getting upset and then I lose my temper. I don't mean to do it. Honestly. I am sorry. You've had a horrible time since I've been here."

Emma didn't answer. It was true. She had had a horrible time since her cousin had arrived. But Emma didn't want to make Alice feel even worse than she already felt.

"Come back to the Grove, Alice," said Nikki. "A lot of us have been through the same sort of thing as you're going through. We'll be on your side. We want to help."

"Why should you want to help? After what I've done."

Nikki smiled. "Because we know what it's like."

"Do you think they really might forgive me?"

"Some of us already have," said Nikki.

Alice hesitated. "Alright," she said. "I'll try."

The back door slammed, startling the three girls.

"It's Mum," said Emma, looking at her watch.

They heard the door between the kitchen and the hallway being opened.

"Emma, are you up there?" shouted Emma's mum from the bottom of the stairs.

"Yes," said Emma.

"Is Alice with you?"

"Yes," said Emma again. "And Nikki."

Loud footsteps sounded on the stairs. Emma's mum opened the door. She looked angry.

"Had a good day, have you?"

"Yes," said Emma cautiously.

"Been at the Grove?"

"Yes," said Emma once more. It was true, she had been at the Grove.

"And what about you, Alice?" said Emma's mum, staring directly at her niece. "Have you been at the Grove?"

Alice knew there was no point in even trying to lie. She could see perfectly well that Emma's mum had discovered the truth.

"No," she said quietly, "I haven't."

"No, you haven't, have you? But you told me this morning that you were going to the Grove."

"Yes, I know, but I…"

"Don't bother Alice. Don't even try to explain. You lied to me, and that's one thing I will not put up with. Well, I've had enough. I'm not having you ruining Emma's holiday and making everyone miserable. I'm phoning your dad tonight and he can come and take you home."

Alice tried to speak again. "But..."

"I don't want to hear about it, Alice. We've tried to help. All of us. But you just don't want to be helped."

"But I do. I..."

"Go downstairs, Emma," said Emma's mum before Alice could finish. "And you too, Nikki. I'm sorry you had to hear this."

Emma tried to speak up in Alice's defence. "Mum..."

"Just go downstairs. Now."

Emma's mum waited until her daughter and Nikki had left the room. "I've got to collect your uncle from work," she said to Alice. "When I get back I'll phone your dad and we'll sort this out once and for all. I suggest you stay up here until then."

The door slammed shut and Emma's mum stomped down the stairs and followed Emma and Nikki into the kitchen.

"And you lied to me, too, Emma," she said angrily. "You know how I feel about telling lies."

"I'm sorry, Mum," said Emma. "I didn't want to."

"No," said her mum, beginning to calm down, "I know you didn't. But you did and you shouldn't have done it."

"How did you find out?" asked Emma.

"I thought I'd give you a lift home so I stopped at the Grove. Regina and Laura were just coming down the drive. They didn't mean to tell me, they thought I already knew. They were worried about you. They said you'd hardly spoken to them today. That's how I found out."

She went to the door. "I'm going to pick your dad up," she said. "Just leave her alone until we get back." And with that, she went out.

"What a mess," said Emma.

Alice sat in Emma's bedroom and sobbed. It was no use. She couldn't put things right. Even when she wanted to. Even when she was ready to try. She went to the wardrobe, opened the doors and grabbed her suitcase from the top shelf. She pulled open the zip and began flinging her clothes inside. In less than a minute it was full. Alice fastened the zip and put on her coat.

Emma and Nikki heard her coming down the stairs. They watched in amazement as Alice burst into the room and struggled towards the back door with the heavy case, crashing and banging into chairs and cupboards as she went.

"Alice…?" said Emma.

"I'm going home," said Alice before Emma could finish.

"But you can't," said Emma. "You can't just go."

"Can't I?" said Alice, pausing by the door. "I'm going home. To my real home. To my mum. You'd better tell your mum and dad I'll be catching the train."

"But Alice…"

"Don't worry, I'll be alright. If anyone cares!"

She opened the door and went out.

Emma went to get up. "I'll have to stop her…"

"No, let me go," said Nikki. "Stay here."

Nikki jumped up and ran out. She saw Alice walking towards the bus stop, but slowly, constantly switching her suitcase from one hand to the other. Nikki quickly caught her up.

"Can I talk to you?" she said. "Please?"

"Do what you like," said Alice, stopping to switch the case again. "It won't make any difference, I'm going." She started walking again.

Nikki walked at her side. "I know how you're feeling."

"Do you?" said Alice. "I doubt it."

"It's like nobody understands you," said Nikki. "Nobody really listens to how you're feeling. Nobody talks to you. Or explains. When you need them to. Isn't it?"

Alice stopped, put down the case and picked it up with the other hand. She began walking again. "Something like that," she said.

"My parents split up when I was four," said Nikki. "I lived with my mum and Greg stayed with Dad. My mum got married again. I thought he was alright at first, her new bloke, then he started…"

Alice was walking more slowly, listening closely to what Nikki was saying.

"He what?"

"He started beating me up."

Alice stopped. She turned and looked at Nikki. "I didn't know."

Nikki shrugged. "Why should you?" she said. "It's not something I talk about very much."

Alice let the suitcase rest on the ground. "What happened?"

"It's alright now. They sent him to prison."

"I'm sorry," said Alice. "It must have been terrible."

Nikki smiled. "That's not why I told you."

"Why, then?" asked Alice.

"I just wanted you to stop walking," said Nikki with a smile.

Alice returned the smile.

"I came to live with my dad," said Nikki. "Everyone tried to be nice to me. To protect me. My dad, my step-mum, Maggie, even my real mum when it came to it, in court. But I didn't want them to be nice, I wanted them to be real."

Alice nodded and Nikki continued. "I didn't want to be treated like a kid. I didn't want them to go around pretending it hadn't happened, or that they couldn't mention it because it might upset me. That's what upset me, playing happy families, pretending everything was normal when it wasn't." Nikki paused. "They think we can't take the truth, don't they?" she added.

Alice nodded. "What's it like now?"

"It's better," said Nikki. "It's not perfect but it's better. Maggie's good, she understands."

"My dad won't talk and my mum… she can't, not about how I'm feeling, anyway," said Alice.

"What about your dad's girlfriend?" said Nikki.

"I don't know. I don't really know her."

"Maybe you should try to get to know her."

Alice looked at the suitcase standing on the pavement.

"You can't run away from it, Alice," said Nikki. "I tried but it doesn't work. You have to face up to it."

Nikki reached down and picked up Alice's suitcase. "Come back with me, Alice," she said. "Come back and sort it out with Emma's parents. And then come back to the Grove. You can do it."

Alice looked back down the road to Emma's house and then at Nikki.

YOU CHOOSE DOES ALICE GO BACK?

YES GO TO PAGE 134

NO GO TO THE NEXT PAGE

Alice reached for the suitcase and took it from Nikki's hand.

"I'm sorry," she said. "I can't. I just can't."

"But what about Emma? And her parents? And what about Ben?"

"I've caused them all enough trouble. I'm going home."

"But…"

"I'm going, Nikki," said Alice. "But thanks for trying." She turned to go. "Goodbye, Nikki."

"Alice, wait!"

Alice stopped. "I've made up my mind."

"I know you have," said Nikki. "But let me carry the case with you. Just to the bus stop."

Alice smiled and allowed Nikki to take one of the handles. She had made up her mind. She knew she was running away from one set of problems and that there would be another set to face when she got home. The telephones would have been ringing and both her parents would know everything. But all that could be faced later. Alice was scared, but at least she had made a decision. She was going home.

They didn't have to wait long for the bus. It squealed to a standstill and the doors slid open.

"Getting on this time, are we?" said a voice.

Nikki peered into the bus and immediately recognised the driver who had stopped earlier. He had obviously recognised her, too.

"I'm not," said Nikki, "but my friend is. I think." She turned and looked at Alice. "Are you certain?"

Alice nodded. "Goodbye, Nikki. And tell Emma I'm sorry. I'm really sorry." She stepped on to the bus, the doors closed and the bus pulled away in the direction of the city.

"Now what do I tell them?" said Nikki.

On the opposite side of the road stood a telephone box. Nikki thought for a moment. Then she crossed the road, went into the phone box and picked up the receiver.

Emma's parents had just walked into the kitchen at their home. They were still wearing their coats and were both staring at their daughter.

Ever since Nikki had run after Alice, Emma had been desperately trying to think of a way to explain this latest crisis to her parents.

"Alice has walked out. She's catching the train back to her mum's. She says don't worry, she'll be alright." It didn't sound very good but it was the truth and Emma didn't want to lie to her mum again.

So as soon as the back door opened, Emma launched into her story. It took just a few seconds and, for a few seconds more, both Emma's parents stood in stunned silence.

"You should have stopped her," said her mum at last.

"Mum!"

"Well, did you try?"

"Be fair, love," said Emma's dad. "If Alice was determined to walk out, Emma could hardly have forced her to stay. How long ago did all this happen, Emma?"

"About fifteen minutes. Just after mum left."

"We'll have to go and look for her," said Emma's mum. "We can't let her just wander around the town."

"She's not wandering around," said Emma. "She said she was going to the station."

"So she said. But how do we know that for sure? She could go anywhere. She could do anything."

Emma's mum turned to her husband. "I'll phone my brother."

"Look hang on, hang on. We don't want to worry him. Not yet. Alice could walk back through the door any…"

He stopped. The back door was opening. But it was Nikki.

"Oh, sorry," she said, seeing Emma's parents. "I should have knocked."

"Don't worry about that," said Emma's mum anxiously. "Where is she?"

"I couldn't stop her," said Nikki. "She's gone to the station."

"Are you sure?"

"I watched her get on the bus."

"Right," said Emma's mum. "I'm phoning her dad."

• • • • •

Alice stood at the ticket office. She pushed some cash under the glass partition and then scooped up the ticket that was handed through to her in exchange.

"Can you tell me where the phones are please?" she said to the woman on the other side of the window.

She pointed. "They're over there. Just keep going. You'll come to them."

"Thanks." Alice put her ticket into her coat pocket and then reached down for her suitcase. It seemed to be getting heavier and heavier. The busy station made Alice feel lonely and homesick, she would be glad to get on to the train, but she had to speak to her mum first.

During the bus journey Alice decided that she must at least begin to explain things before she got home. And she would need to be met at the station when her train arrived.

Alice was nearly out of money. She hadn't expected to have to buy a train ticket. She fumbled in her pockets, found some coins, went into the phone booth and dialled her home number.

The telephone rang three times and then the answering machine clicked into action. Alice heard her mum's voice and felt even more homesick. The message ended and the tone sounded.

Alice hesitated. Perhaps her mum was at home but hadn't picked up the phone. Sometimes she did that, just to find out who was making the call.

"Mum," said Alice, "are you there?" She wasn't. Alice didn't know what else to say – she couldn't possibly try to explain in an answering machine message.

She put down the receiver, wishing that she hadn't spoken at all. Her mum would worry when she heard those few words. But she still needed someone to meet her at the station. She would have to phone her dad.

Alice was dreading speaking to her dad. He would definitely have spoken to Emma's mum. But there was no other choice.

She took another coin from her pocket, dropped it into the slot and dialled her dad's number.

The phone rang just once. "Hello?"

It wasn't Alice's dad. It was Cheryl.

"Hello," said Alice hesitantly. She still found it difficult to use Cheryl's name. She hardly ever did, even though both her dad and Cheryl had told her she should.

"Alice? Is that you?"

"Yes," said Alice. "Is Dad there?"

"No, he's not," said Cheryl. "He had to work overtime. But your aunt called."

"Oh."
"Where are you, Alice?"
"I'm at the station. The train leaves in about five minutes."
"Have you phoned your mum?"
"Yes, but she's not there."
"Get on the train, Alice," said Cheryl. "I'll pick you up at the station."
"But I want to go home."
"I'll take you home."
"But..."
"Don't worry, I'll take you home. Just go to the platform and get on the train."
"Alright, I will. Bye." Alice went to replace the receiver but then stopped. She put it back to her ear. "Thanks," she said. But she was too late. She heard the buzzing of the dialling tone. Cheryl had gone.
Cheryl and Alice's mum had never met and her mum said often that she didn't want to meet Cheryl. Ever.
Alice walked towards the platform thinking that if Cheryl drove her home and her mum had returned then they were bound to meet. Cheryl couldn't just drop her off and drive away. Everything was becoming more and more difficult.
"Alice!" The shout echoed around the tall station building.
Alice turned and saw Ben running towards her.
He stopped, red-faced and breathless. "I thought I'd miss you," he said as he reached her side.
"Ben? Why are you... how did you know?"
"Nikki called me. I ran. Alice don't go. Stay. I want you to stay. We can sort it out."
"I can't, Ben. Nikki shouldn't have called you. I told her I've got to go home."
"But I want you to stay."
"I can't!"
"Alice, I really like you."
They stared at each other. Unsure of what to do next. Or of what to say.
"And... and I like you, Ben," Alice said at last. "I think you're really nice. But I've got to go home. I want to go home. I'm sorry."
Ben knew then that there was nothing more that he could say. Alice wouldn't change her mind, not even for him.

"Come to the train with me?" she asked softly.

Ben nodded and took Alice's case from her hands. They walked on to the platform and saw that the train was already there, almost ready to depart. They hurried to the nearest carriage and Ben opened the door and placed the suitcase inside.

"I'm sorry, Ben," said Alice. "Maybe I'll come back, when things are better."

She reached for Ben's hands, took them in hers and then leaned towards him. They kissed. Briefly.

Alice smiled. "Goodbye, Ben," she whispered.

She climbed on to the train, pulled the heavy door shut, grabbed her suitcase and ran into the carriage. There was a window-seat free. She threw herself into the seat and the train began to move away. Ben watched as Alice blew a last kiss towards him. And then she was gone.

Ben was alone on the platform. He didn't want to move. He didn't understand. Why wouldn't she stay? With him? He would have helped her. It would have been alright.

"Ben?"

Ben turned and looked back down the platform. Emma and her parents were running towards him.

"You're too late," he said as they came to a standstill. "She's gone."

• • • • •

Cheryl was waiting by the station exit. She smiled. "Hello, Alice."

"Hello," replied Alice, and then she added, "Cheryl."

The train ride from Newcastle to Alice's home town had not taken very long but throughout the journey Alice had grown more and more anxious.

"The car's outside. Shall I take your case?"

"It's alright, thanks, I can manage."

They loaded the case into the boot of the car and drove off into the darkening evening.

"Your mum called. Just after you," said Cheryl. "She was worried when she heard your message."

"I thought she would be," said Alice "I shouldn't have said anything."

"I'm glad you did."

Alice was puzzled. "Are you? Why?"

Cheryl nodded. "Your mum and me had a chat."

"Oh?"

"It was the first time we'd talked properly. We've never said more than two or three words to each other before."

"Does Dad know?"

"He's still at work. I haven't spoken to him."

Alice thought for a few moments. "Why didn't Mum come and pick me up?"

Cheryl laughed. "I was wondering when you'd ask that."

"Is she angry with me?"

"No-one's angry with you, Alice. We're more angry with ourselves." She paused before continuing. "How do you feel about having a proper talk?"

"What, now?"

"Yes."

"But I've got to go home."

"I know. That's what I mean."

"What?" said Alice in amazement. "With Mum, too?"

"Yes."

"But you've never..."

"I know. We've never met. But if we can't talk to each other we can hardly talk to you, can we?"

Alice could hardly imagine it. Her mum and Cheryl, sitting together, and talking.

They travelled in silence for a few minutes and Alice gazed out through the windscreen. It was completely dark by now but the streetlamps and car headlights illuminated the darkness. Alice realised that she and Cheryl had also never really spoken to each other. Not properly. And this was the first time they had ever been alone together.

"We've never really talked, have we?" said Cheryl.

Alice gave a slight laugh.

"What?" said Cheryl.

"I was just thinking that."

"So it's about time we did."

They were driving along a main road, lined on both sides with shops and garages and supermarkets. Some were open, it was still early evening, but Alice felt as though the day had lasted for ever. They reached a junction and Cheryl turned the car into a smaller, less busy street. On either side were houses and flats.

"You'll have to start giving me directions now," said Cheryl.

"Third right off this road," said Alice.

"It might not be easy," said Cheryl. "This meeting. Not at first, at least."

"I know," answered Alice.

"But we've got to try. We've got to listen to each other."

"Yeah. This is the turning."

Cheryl turned the car again.

"Now you go to the end and turn left," said Alice.

"There's something I want you to know before we arrive," said Cheryl.

Alice waited and Cheryl continued. "I want you to know that I'll never try and come between you and your dad. He loves you so much, I know he's not always brilliant at showing it, but he's always telling me how much you mean to him."

"Is he?"

"Always. And I'm glad he loves you so much. I wouldn't love a man who didn't love his daughter, would I?"

"I suppose not."

"I want us to be friends, Alice. I really do. But we can't force it to happen. We can want it, and hope that we really grow to like each other. I think we will. We've got something in common to start with."

"Have we?" asked Alice.

"Well, we both love your dad, don't we?"

They reached the junction and Cheryl turned the car into the street where Alice lived.

"It's just down there, on the right, by that lamp post."

Cheryl took a deep breath as she stopped the car at the kerb side. "Right, here we go then," she said, switching off the engine and turning out the lights. "Your dad'll be surprised when he hears about this."

They got out of the car.

"I'm a bit nervous," said Alice.

"So am I," Cheryl replied. "And I bet your mum is, too."

• • • • •

"Not another list?" said Laura.

"Someone has to do it, Laura," said Regina. "It's important. Someone has to decide what food and drink we're having at the party. These things don't just happen on their own, you know. Sometimes I think if it wasn't for me nothing would ever get done at this place."

"Mmm," said Laura.

Regina picked up a pencil and studied the blank sheet at the top of her notepad. "Sausages, burgers," she said aloud as she wrote. "I suppose we'll have to get some vegeburgers for people like Nikki. What else?"

Laura didn't answer. She was worried about Emma. And Alice. She had been worrying about both of them ever since she and Regina had spoken to Emma's mum on the previous evening.

Regina glanced up from her list. "Laura, what else do you think...? She stopped. Emma had walked into the room. And she was smiling.

"Emma," said Laura, jumping up from her chair and rushing over to her friend. "We're really sorry. We didn't mean to say anything. We didn't mean to split on you. Or on Alice."

"It's alright, Laura," said Emma. "I know you didn't."

Regina joined them. "What's happened? Where is Alice?"

"Let's sit down, shall we?" said Emma. "I'll tell you all about it."

They went back to the table and sat down.

"What are you writing?" asked Emma, glancing at Regina's list.

"Oh, come on, Emma," said Regina impatiently, "what's happened?"

"She's gone home," said Emma with a sigh. "She went back on the train last night. Nikki tried to stop her outside my house, but she wouldn't listen. Then Nikki phoned Ben and he tried to stop her at the station. But it was no use, she wouldn't change her mind."

Laura and Regina gasped.

"We went to the station, too," said Emma.

"Who?" asked Laura.

"Mum and Dad and me. But we were too late, she'd gone. We met Ben on the platform. He was really upset."

Laura and Regina exchanged wide-eyed looks of amazement.

"Alice's mum phoned last night to say that she was there and she was alright," continued Emma. "That's all we know."

Regina and Laura paused to consider the sensational news. "Are you glad she's gone?" asked Laura.

"I don't know," said Emma. "It makes things easier, I suppose. But I wish it could have been different. She's nice really."

Regina frowned.

"Honestly, Regina, she is," said Emma. "But no-one at the Grove will think of her that way." She glanced again at Regina's list. "What are you doing?"

"We're making a list of food and drink we'll need for the party," said Regina. "D'you want to help?"

Emma nodded. "It'll be nice to do something normal for a change. What have you got so far?"

"Sausages and burgers. But tell us about what happened with Ben. At the station. What did he say?"

"Regina, you said this list was important," said Laura.

"It is important," said Regina. "But it can wait."

Emma laughed. "I'll tell you while we're working on the list," she said.

The next few days passed quickly. The grounds of the Grove were transformed. The huge bonfire was built, a barbecue, tables and benches were set up and a temporary stage, made of wooden planks and crates, stood ready for the entertainment.

Regina and her gang went on shopping trips and returned with cardboard boxes and plastic bags full of food and drink.

Last-minute rehearsals took place behind closed doors. Bradley had reluctantly accepted that he was never going to find someone willing to be sawn in half, even if it wasn't for real. He announced that he was now planning another trick that involved pulling a white rabbit and several pigeons out of a hat, but Nikki told him that if he did, she would report him to the RSPCA for being cruel to animals.

"It's not cruel. I'm a magician, that's what magicians do," Bradley moaned. "No-one wants to be sawn in half and I can't use animals. I suppose you want me to do boring old card tricks."

"Do what you like," Nikki told him. "Just leave animals out of it. How would you like to be pulled out of a hat?"

Don't Waste Energy Day finally arrived. It was bright and dry, but cold.

"It definitely won't rain," Regina told Tina. "I watched the weather forecast on telly last night."

Regina's list of rules and regulations was prominently displayed on the noticeboard, even though it was a little difficult to see. The Grove was in semi-darkness. Half the lights were switched off and so were the drinks machine and the television. The heating had been turned down, doors were closed and taps were turned firmly off. Many of the Grovers sat around in the general room – feeling miserable.

"How am I supposed to rehearse?" said Bradley. "My hands are so cold I keep dropping my cards."

"Not a lot of fun, is it?" said Bill. Laura was sitting near to him. He peered through the gloom. "Is that you, Laura?"

"Ha, ha," said Laura sarcastically. "You can see me perfectly well. Anyway, Regina's right, this is serious."

"What is?"

"Well, just think what it'd be like if we didn't have electricity and gas."

"Yeah but we have got it, and it's dark and we're freezing," said Bradley. "Maybe we should go and light the bonfire now."

"Don't you dare," said Regina as she marched into the room. "You've only got to put up with it for one day. That's all."

Barry and Joe walked into the room. "There's a van coming up the drive, Regina," said Barry.

"So?" said Regina. "What's that got to do with me?"

"It's got *Byker Post* written on the side," said Barry. "Maybe it's the…"

"It's the posters," yelled Regina and she rushed from the room. She was waiting by the front door before the van had even stopped.

"Have you got our posters?" she asked the driver the moment he opened the van door.

"I've got a package. For Miss Regina O'Hagan," said the driver with a smile.

"That's me."

"I thought it might be." He went to the back of the van and brought out the large package. Regina directed him to the general room where he dumped the heavy posters on the edge of the stage.

"Sign there," he said to Regina, offering her a sheet of paper and a pen.

"D'you want my autograph?" said Regina.

"Something like that," said the driver. "You have to sign for the parcel before I can leave it."

"Oh," said Regina. She proudly signed her name and the driver departed.

"Get some scissors, someone," ordered Regina.

"I already have," said Laura. The Grovers crowded around as Laura cut the cord tied round the package and pulled out the top poster.

"Brilliant," said Regina. "You've all got to help take them round the town tomorrow, but we'll put one up in here for now."

She took the poster from Laura and walked to the wall opposite the doorway. "We'll put it here," she said, "so that everyone can see it as they come in."

"I doubt it," said Bill. "It's too dark in here to see anything."

• • • • •

The party was going well. Very well. The bonfire had blazed for more than an hour and was beginning to die down. Candles burned brightly in jars on the tables, and lamps with more candles hung from some of the closest trees.

Ollie and Liam had amazed the Grovers by offering to be barbecue chefs. And apart from a few blackened sausages and burnt burgers, the food was good.

"There's nothing like a good burger," said Nat to Liam as she munched on a burger he had prepared.

"D'you reckon?" asked Liam.

"Yeah," said Nat. She laughed. "And this one's nothing like a good burger."

"Very funny," said Liam. "You finished it, though. There's one left. D'you want it?"

"Yeah," said Nat, offering her empty plate. "Why not?"

"Come on," said Liam, "I've had enough of cooking. Let's go and see Mr Jolly Wally."

Mr Jolly Wally was the name that Bradley had first used when he began his clowning and magic act. But Bradley had decided he needed a more sophisticated name for the party and had decided to appear as 'The Magnificent Bradley'.

Most of the Grovers sat on benches watching The Magnificent

Bradley perform his final trick. Sadly for Bradley there was no sawing involved, no white rabbits and not even a single pigeon, but as his magician's cloak swirled around, he put both hands up to his mouth and appeared to pull out a long string of coloured handkerchiefs. The Grovers clapped and cheered as Bradley took a slow and extravagant bow.

"Get off!" yelled Liam with a grin, but even he was secretly impressed.

Bradley swept off the stage and Regina swept on to it.

"Thank you, The Magnificent Bradley," she said. "And now, it's time for our top of the bill act. Let's give a real Byker Grove welcome to Karen, Sita and Cher!"

The Grovers burst into applause as the three girls ran on to the stage, wearing matching dresses in blue, yellow and red.

They began to sing, and as their sweet harmonies filled the evening air, the grounds of Byker Grove were bathed in firelight and candlelight. Everyone watched and listened in absolute silence as the shadows cast by the bonfire flickered across the stage. At the end of the song every one of the Grovers stood and applauded loudly – everyone but Ben.

Ben wasn't in a party mood. He was missing Alice. He'd been missing her all week, ever since she'd gone home. As the cheers and applause reverberated around the grounds of Byker Grove, Ben was thinking of the last moments he had spent with Alice. They had stood together on the station platform. They had kissed. Just one, brief kiss. And then she was gone. Since then, Ben had heard nothing from Alice. Not a letter. Not a phone call. Not a word.

"Thanks very much," said Karen from the stage. "We're going to do a slow one now, so if any of you lads fancy asking someone to dance, now's your chance."

Karen, Cher and Sita started their second song and, gradually, some of the boys were brave enough to ask the girls to dance. Bill and Laura were first, then Liam and Nat, Ollie and Teraise, Nikki and Matt, Joe and Emma, and even Regina and Bradley.

"Aren't you gonna dance with someone?"

Ben turned. He hadn't heard Tina approaching. He shrugged. "I'm not in the mood."

"Go on," said Tina. "It's so romantic. Look, Claire's on her own over there."

Ben looked over to where Claire sat on one of the benches. She was alone.

"Go on," said Tina again. "It's only a dance."

Ben hesitated, but not for long. Tina was right. Why shouldn't he ask Claire to dance? It was only a dance. And anyway, Alice hadn't contacted him. She hadn't written, or called. She'd probably already forgotten all about him.

"Yeah, alright," he said. "Why not?"

He walked over to Claire and a few moments later they were dancing, their arms wrapped around each other.

Emma and Joe were dancing nearby. As the song continued Emma watched as Claire rested her head on Ben's shoulders and he pulled her a little closer.

"So much for Alice," said Emma softly.

• • • • •

Emma was sitting in the kitchen, eating a slice of toast and reading a letter she had just received from Alice.

"She says things are much better," said Emma.

"That's good," said her mum, who sat opposite.

"She had a really good talk with her mum and Cheryl."

"How did they get on?"

Emma looked up from the letter. "She doesn't say, but at least they talked. That's a start, isn't it?"

"Mmm," said Emma's mum, as she sipped from a mug of coffee she was holding in both hands. "What about Uncle David?"

Emma studied the letter again. "She says he still finds it difficult to talk, but that he's trying. And she says that she's decided she just has to get on with things and stop worrying so much."

"That's good," said Emma's mum, finishing her coffee. "I'm sure they'll sort it out. They all want to, that's the most important thing."

"And there's a message for you," said Emma as she read the final page of the letter. "She says to tell you how sorry she is for everything we had to put up with while she was here. She hopes you'll forgive her and that she'll be a different person the next time you see her."

"Let's hope so," said Emma's mum with a smile.

"PS. How's Ben?" read Emma. "Send him my love and tell him I'm sorry I haven't been in contact and that I do miss him."

Emma folded the letter and slid it back into the envelope. "I don't think Ben's missing her. You should have seen him with Claire at the party."

"Oh, well," said her mum. "It was just a little holiday romance. Everyone has those."

"Do they?" asked Emma.

"Of course they do."

"Did you?"

Her mum laughed. "One or two. I've had my moments."

"Have you?" asked Emma with a shocked look on her face.

"Don't look so surprised," said her mum. "And I don't know why you're sounding so amazed. I was young once, too, you know. I still am young."

"Yeah, right."

"Watch it, you."

"Tell me about them, then."

"What?"

"Your holiday romances."

"I'll tell you when you're older."

"Oh, Mum!"

"Oh, alright. Well, there was this boy I met when I went on holiday to Spain with my parents."

"How old were you?"

"About your age. No, a bit older."

"Yeah, go on."

"Well, he was really nice and…" She stopped.

"Oh, come on, Mum."

Emma's mum switched on the kettle. "I'll just make another cup of coffee, then I can tell you properly. But it's our secret, mind. Don't tell your dad. We don't want to make him jealous, do we?"

THE END

Alice reached for the suitcase and took it from Nikki's hand.

"Alright," she said. "If you really think it's worth it, I'll try. We'll go back."

"It's the right thing to do, Alice," said Nikki. "I'm sure it is. Let's get this suitcase indoors before Emma's mum and dad get back. We don't want them to see it."

They turned back towards Emma's house but had taken only a few steps when Alice stopped again.

"We're too late," she said. "Look."

"Oh, no," said Nikki.

A car was pulling up outside the house. The girls stood on the pavement with the suitcase between them as Emma's parents got out of the car.

"I think they've seen it," said Alice.

They had, and Emma's mum was not pleased. She strode angrily up to her niece. "What on earth are you doing now, Alice? Why have you got your case? Where d'you think you're going?"

"I'm not going anywhere, Auntie Jackie," said Alice. "I was going home. To my mum's. But Nikki stopped me."

"Oh, Alice," said her aunt with an exasperated sigh. "What are we going to do with you?"

"I'm sorry. It's just that everything keeps going wrong and I didn't know what else to do."

Alice was close to tears again, and Emma's mum could see that her niece desperately needed kind rather than harsh words. She put a comforting arm around Alice's shoulders and squeezed her gently. "Come on," she said with a smile. "Come inside and we'll try to sort this out."

Emma heard them walking towards the back door. She heard her mum and dad but for a brief moment she didn't realise that Alice and Nikki were with them. She had been panicking over how she could possibly tell her parents that Alice had walked out. The door opened and Emma's dad walked in with the suitcase. Next came Emma's mum, and then Alice and Nikki. Emma breathed a huge sigh of relief.

Alice smiled timidly at her cousin. "I'm sorry, Emma," she said, and then turned immediately to her aunt and uncle. "I know I've been awful, ever since I got here. And I've done some really stupid things. I'm so sorry. For everything. I was going home because I couldn't face any of you."

"Alice, you can't just run away every time something goes wrong," said Emma's mum.

"I know," Alice replied. "Nikki made me realise that."

"Well, what are you going to do about it?"

"Will you let me stay?" Alice asked softly. "Will you let me try again? I want to go back to the Grove to apologise and ask everyone to give me another chance. They probably won't, but I want to ask."

Alice looked at her aunt, and then at her uncle, and then back at her aunt, who looked at her husband, who was still standing in the middle of the kitchen with Alice's suitcase in his hands.

"What do you think?" said Emma's mum.

He finally put the suitcase down on to the floor. "I think she should stay," he said. "I think we should give her another chance. You won't let us down, will you, Alice?"

"I won't," said Alice urgently. "Really, I won't."

"Alright," said Emma's mum. "Make sure you don't. And don't let Emma and Nikki down, either." She smiled. "You'd better go and unpack that suitcase, hadn't you? And I need a cup of tea!"

Nikki had been standing quietly by the door, unsure if she should stay or go, but now she knew it was definitely time for her to leave. "I'll be off then," she said.

"Oh, Nikki, thanks so much," said Emma's mum. "You've been fantastic. We're very grateful." She glanced at her niece. "Aren't we, Alice?"

"Very grateful," replied Alice as she crossed the room to hug Nikki.

As soon as Nikki had gone, Emma and Alice went upstairs to unpack the suitcase.

Emma's dad waited until he heard the bedroom door close. "Well, at least that's sorted, then," he said.

"No it isn't," said Emma's mum. "We've got to do something."

"Do? We just said what we were doing. We told her she could stay."

"But we can't just leave it like that," said Emma's mum. "We can't just pretend these things are not happening. It could happen again. What if she goes to the Grove tomorrow and they don't let her back? She might run off again. Or do something worse."

"What d'you mean, worse?"

"I don't know. But we just can't leave it like this." She went to the telephone. "I'm going to phone my brother. Alice is his daughter.

This is his problem and he can't just leave it to us to sort out. I used to have to sort out David's problems when we were kids, but I'm not doing it now. It's up to him to help his daughter."

Emma's mum picked up the telephone. "This might be a long conversation," she said to her husband.

"Right," said Emma's dad. "I'll make the tea then, shall I?"

• • • • •

Nikki also spent a long time on the telephone that evening, but she made a number of calls. First she phoned Ben, and when they had spoken for a few minutes, she asked him to tell Liam some of what she'd said.

Next she called Teraise, and she asked her not to mention any of their conversation to her cousin, Regina. Then she phoned Karen, and then Cher, and then Nat and her brother Ollie. Finally, she called Sita.

She asked them all to come to her house the following morning. She didn't tell them what their meeting was to be about, just that it was important. Everyone agreed to be there.

By ten o'clock the following morning the living room at Nikki's house looked more like the general room at Byker Grove. Every chair was taken and so was most of the floor.

"So what are we doing here?" said Nat, glancing dismissively in the direction of Cher and Karen. "We're not all exactly the best of friends, are we?"

"No, but we've all got something in common. Most of us, at least," answered Nikki.

"And what's that, then?"

"We've all had problems with parents. Splitting up, divorcing, leaving."

"Sita hasn't," said Cher.

"I said most of us," said Nikki. "But I asked Sita to come because she's the most sensible person at the Grove."

"I wouldn't say that," said Nat.

Sita smiled but didn't respond.

Nikki's brother Greg was also in the room. "So what if we have got it in common? It's not exactly unusual to have problems with parents, is it? What d'you want us to do? Form a club?"

"No, Greg, I don't."

"Well, get to the point, then."

Nikki told them everything that had happened the previous evening. She told them about the row between Alice and her aunt, and about how Alice had packed her case and walked out, and about how she had finally managed to convince Alice to stay.

"Well, that's very interesting," said Liam when Nikki had finished, "but what's it got to do with us?"

"I told her that she had to come back to the Grove today," said Nikki. "I said she had to apologise to everyone for what she's done and ask for another chance."

"Oh, I get it," said Nat. "And you want us all to be on her side when she turns up. Because we can sympathise with her. Because we understand what it's like."

"Yeah," said Nikki. "That's right. Her mum and dad only split up a few months ago and her dad's got a new girlfriend."

"They usually do," said Karen.

"Alice has been having a really bad time," Nikki continued.

"Yeah, well, maybe we do understand, and I'm sure we all sympathise," said Teraise. "Most of us, at least. But that doesn't mean to say we can just forget what she did."

"Why not?" said Nikki. "We all know how bad she must have been feeling to do something like that."

"She didn't mean to do it," added Ben. "Not really. She was just angry about everything."

"Yeah, well, you would say that," said Ollie. "You fancy her."

"That's got nothing to do with it."

"Yeah, right."

"Has she put you up to this?" asked Liam, looking at Nikki. "Did she ask you to get us here so you could talk us round?"

"No," said Nikki. "She knows nothing about it. This was my idea."

"Sounds like one of your ideas," said Greg.

"Why didn't you want me to tell Regina?" asked Teraise.

"Regina's just a kid," said Nikki. "And anyway, this whole poster competition thing was her idea. She's taken it personally. She doesn't like Alice."

"You can't really blame her," said Cher.

"No, I don't," said Nikki. "But I just think that if we show Regina and everyone else at the Grove that we're prepared to forgive and forget, then they might, too."

The room was silent as they considered what Nikki had said. Nikki looked hopefully from face to face. Ollie shrugged and so did Nat, Cher looked at Karen, Ben smiled and nodded, Liam gazed out through the window, Teraise seemed to be studying the material of the chair she was sitting on, and Greg looked as though he didn't care one way or the other.

"I think Nikki's right," said Sita.

"You're only saying that because she said you were sensible," said Nat.

"No I'm not. She is right. We all do things wrong. All of us, even you, Nat."

Nat shrugged. "Yeah, but if you can't do the time you shouldn't do the crime."

"What?" said Teraise.

"I heard it in a film."

"Yeah, but what does it mean?"

"It means, that if you can't… Oh, forget it."

"It means that if you're going to do something wrong you've got to be prepared to accept the consequences," said Sita.

"I could have told her that," said Nat.

"Yeah, well, that's true enough, though, isn't it?" said Teraise.

"But what's the point in us punishing Alice when she's already going through a bad time," Sita continued. "I think we should give her another chance."

"I agree," said Karen.

"You would," said Nat.

"Well, don't you?" said Cher.

Everyone turned to look at Nat. Nat waited. She did agree, she did think they should give Alice a second chance, but she was going to make the others wait for her answer.

"Well?" asked Nikki.

"Yeah," said Nat at last. "Why not?"

Nikki smiled. "And does everyone else agree, too?"

"I do," said Teraise.

"Yeah," said Liam.

"S'pose so," said Ollie.

Greg nodded.

"Brilliant," said Ben.

"But it's not us you've really got to convince," said Teraise to Nikki. "It's Tina. She's the one who decides whether or not Alice is allowed back."

"I know that," said Nikki. "And I will convince her, as long as you lot are on my side."

"You probably will," said Cher as she stood up to leave. "If you can convince Nat, I reckon you can convince anyone."

• • • • •

It was late when Alice woke up that morning. She hadn't realised how tired she had been the night before, but when she finally opened her eyes and looked over to Emma's bed she saw that it was empty.

Alice lay in bed and dozed, half awake and half asleep, sometimes thinking about all that had happened during her traumatic week at the Grove and sometimes drifting into dreams.

She dreamt about Emma, and about her aunt and uncle, and about Nikki and Ben and Regina, and then she dreamt about her dad. In her dream she could hear his voice, he was talking softly. And there were other voices. She could hear the voices but she couldn't quite hear what they were saying.

Alice sat up. She was wide awake. She wasn't dreaming. She could hear her dad's voice – he was there, downstairs, talking to her aunt and uncle. Alice leapt out of bed and ran to the top of the stairs.

"Dad?" she called. "Dad?"

The door to the kitchen opened and Alice's dad stepped into the hallway and looked up the stairs.

He smiled. "Hello, love," he said.

"Dad! What are you doing here?"

"That's a nice welcome."

"But… why are you here?"

"We'll talk when you're dressed, eh?" said Alice's dad. He smiled again. "Don't worry, everything's fine."

But Alice did worry. She washed and dressed quickly, all the while wondering why her dad had come. Her aunt must have called him. But why? She'd said she could stay. She must have changed her mind. They wanted her to go.

She hurried down the stairs and went into the kitchen. Her dad was alone.

"Where's…?"

"They went out," said Alice's dad. "Just for a while. Come and sit down, Alice. We need to have a talk."

Alice sat opposite her dad. She didn't know what to say or even where to begin.

"I'm sorry, love," said Alice's dad. "I'm so sorry."

"You're sorry?" said Alice slowly. "I'm the one who should be saying sorry."

"No, Alice, it's me. Your aunt told me everything. She called me last night and I said I'd drive over this morning. I couldn't sleep. I've been thinking about it all night, and all the way here."

"Are you really angry with me?"

"I'm angry with myself, Alice. I should never have let it get like this. We should have talked, but you know I've never been much good at talking, not about things that really matter. It's not that I didn't want to, I just don't find it easy."

"I know you don't, Dad," said Alice. "But you wouldn't talk to me and Mum wouldn't either and I've been feeling so… confused about everything."

"I phoned your mum last night."

"Oh," said Alice. "Is she angry?"

"No. She said when you get back we all need to sit down and try to talk things over. Properly."

"And will we, Dad?"

He nodded. "Yeah. We will. I've got to stop treating you as though you were still five years old. I realise that now. At last. I want to put this right, Alice."

He reached across the table and took both Alice's hands in his. "I'd like you to come home, Alice. Today. I want to make a new start. Right now."

"But Auntie Jackie said I could stay."

"You can stay, if you want to. But I'd like you to come home."

Alice looked into her dad's eyes. "Do you, Dad? Really?"

He nodded. "Really."

"I'd better go and pack my case," said Alice. She smiled. "Again."

They stood up and Alice's dad took his daughter in his arms and hugged her. "Go on, then," he said.

Alice turned and went to the door. She started to climb the stairs but then stopped and went back to the doorway. "Dad, can we stop at the Grove on the way home? I want to apologise for what I've done. And I need to say goodbye."

"Of course we can," said her dad. "We'll wait for your aunt and uncle to get back. You need to see them, and Emma too, and then I'll drive you to this Byker Grove. It sounds quite a place from what Emma's been telling me."

"It is," said Alice with a smile, and she hurried up the stairs.

• • • • •

Alice's dad's car came to a standstill in the Grove car park.

"Are you sure it'll be alright?" he asked.

"Yeah, it'll be fine," said Alice as she unfastened her seatbelt and opened the door.

Emma was sitting in the back seat. She leaned forward and kissed her uncle on the cheek. "Bye, Uncle David," she said. "See you soon, I hope."

"Bye, Emma," he replied as Emma got out of the car. "And thanks."

"What for?"

"For being a good cousin."

Alice looked back into the car. "Won't be long, Dad," she said, and she closed the door.

The two girls walked towards the main entrance door of the Grove. Alice had told her dad it would be fine, but she was far from certain that she was right. It might not be fine. It might be awful. But she had to try to put things right at the Grove before she left for good. She had to. For Emma, and for Nikki, and for Ben. And for herself.

They walked through the door and came face to face with Sita, Karen and Cher.

"Hi," said Sita to Alice with a smile. Karen and Cher smiled, too.

Alice was taken aback. The last time she had seen the Grovers nobody had smiled. They had glared at her angrily.

"Oh, hello," she said hesitantly. "D'you know if Tina's in the office?"

"She's in the general room," said Karen. "Regina's boring everyone with her rules and regulations for this saving energy day of hers. We were giving it a miss, but we'll come in if you're going in."

"Oh... right," said Alice. "Well, I need to speak to Regina, too."

She exchanged a nervous look with her cousin and they walked on towards the general room. Sita, Karen and Cher smiled at each other and followed them in.

"...and we've made up a list of rules," Regina was saying. "We'll be putting it on the noticeboard and..." She stopped speaking as she saw Alice and Emma enter the room. But she didn't scowl at Alice, or glare, or even frown. She smiled.

Alice gazed around the room. Most of the Grovers were there. They were looking at her. And most of them were smiling. Nikki was smiling. So was Teraise. Ollie was grinning. Ben's smile was the broadest of all.

"Hello, Alice," said Tina. "We thought you might come back today."

"Did you?" said Alice nervously. "Well, I'm glad there are so many people here because there's something I want to say."

No-one spoke. They just smiled. Alice glanced at her cousin. Emma looked back and shrugged. She was as confused as Alice was at the reaction of the Grovers.

Neither of them knew that Nikki and the others had spoken earlier to Tina about their meeting that morning. Tina had been delighted to hear that they all wanted to forgive Alice and give her another chance.

After that it had simply been a question of persuading everyone else at the Grove. So before Regina's meeting began, Tina had announced that she had something to say.

Most of the young Grovers were easy to convince, especially when they heard that the older members of Byker Grove had already decided that Alice should be forgiven and the ban should be lifted. Regina was the only exception.

"Why should we forgive her?" she argued. "She nearly ruined the posters and she nearly ruined my saving energy day."

"But she didn't ruin it," Tina said. "Everything's going ahead as planned."

"That's not the point," said Regina.

"Regina, you've been telling us all not to waste energy, haven't you?"

"You know I have. It's important."

"I agree. So isn't it a waste of our energy to bear grudges? What Alice did wasn't that terrible. Shouldn't we just forgive and forget?"

Regina paused to consider Tina's words. The other Grovers could almost see her thinking.

"Oh, alright," she said quickly. "But can we get on with my meeting now?"

The Grovers had forgiven Alice before she had even arrived. But Alice didn't know that as she began to make her apology.

"I just want to tell you all that I'm really sorry for what I did. I've never done anything like that before. It was stupid. Everyone's been so nice to me here and I've been horrible."

They were still smiling.

Alice looked at Regina. "And most of all I want to apologise to you, Regina," she said. "I know how much your saving energy day means to you and I nearly spoiled it. I'm very sorry. Honestly."

Regina smiled sweetly. "That's alright, Alice," she said. "I forgive you. I hope the others will, too."

"Oh," said Alice. "Do you?"

Tina laughed. "Everyone forgives you, Alice. Some of your particular friends had a word with us earlier. We'd all like you to come back and enjoy the rest of your holiday. You're still a member of Byker Grove."

"Oh," said Alice again. "But I'm going home."

"What?" said Nikki.

"What?" said Ben.

"Oh, well," said Nat to Nikki. "At least you tried."

Some of the Grovers tried to convince Alice that she should stay, particularly her new-found friend Regina, but Alice told them quickly that she really did want to go home and that her dad was waiting for her in the car park. She thanked them all, for forgiving her, for understanding, for giving her another chance, for everything. And then she left, quickly. She had to. If not, she would have cried. She walked to the doorway with Emma, Nikki and Ben.

Alice hugged her cousin. "It'll be better next time," she said. "Like it used to be."

Emma smiled and nodded. She, too, was close to tears.

Alice turned to Nikki. "You really helped me. I won't forget what you said and what you did. It was special."

"Bye, Alice," said Nikki. "I hope you come back."

Emma and Nikki went back into the Grove as Ben and Alice walked to the edge of the car park.

"You do understand, don't you, Ben?" said Alice. "Why I've got to go home?"

"Yeah," he answered. "I suppose so."

"I'll write, and maybe I'll see you again. Next holiday. Or the one after."

"Yeah," said Ben again. He didn't want her to go.

"Alice..." Ben didn't know quite what to say, so he took one of Alice's hands in his and pulled her gently towards him. Ben meant to kiss Alice on the lips but at the last moment she turned her head slightly and kissed him on the cheek.

"My dad's watching," she whispered. "Next time, though, it'll be different."

"Oh, yeah," Ben replied, glancing towards the car. "Next time. I'll see you then, Alice. I hope."

He turned away and walked back to the Grove.

"Sorry it took so long, Dad," said Alice brightly as she got into the car and fastened her seatbelt. She looked through the window, back towards the Grove. Alice's dad knew there were tears in his daughter's eyes.

"That's alright, love," her dad replied with a smile as he started the engine. "I see you made one particular friend."

"More than one, Dad," Alice whispered, and they drove down the drive and away from Byker Grove.

• • • • •

It was Saturday morning, nearly two weeks later. Alice came downstairs in her dressing gown. Her mum had gone out, but propped against a vase standing on the kitchen table was a letter addressed to Alice. She tore open the envelope, pulled out the letter and began to read:

Dear Alice,

Thanks for your letter. I was really glad to hear that things are starting to get better at home and that you've been able to talk to your mum and dad. It's good that Cheryl's trying to help too. Mum and Dad and me have been thinking about you a lot since you went, so it was great to get your letter.

Mum read it after me (you don't mind, do you?) and she says it's good to know that you're sounding so positive.

You asked me how Regina's saving energy day and the party went. Well, the Grove was freezing and nearly dark. Regina made sure the heating was turned down and half the lights were switched off. It was really gloomy, but Regina kept going around telling us we were doing something very important. I suppose we were really. Most of us were just wanting the day to be over so that we could get on with the party. It was great, I'm really sorry you missed it.

We had this gigantic bonfire and we had candles in jars on all the tables and there were some more candles hanging in the trees. It looked lovely, like something out of a film.

We had loads of food on the barbecue. Ollie and Liam were chefs! They weren't bad, a few of the sausages ended up a bit overdone. And then we had the entertainment – it was excellent.

You remember Bradley, the magician? Remember he wanted to do this trick where he sawed someone in half? Well, surprise, surprise, he didn't find anyone to volunteer. So then he said he wanted to do a trick where he pulled live rabbits and pigeons out of a hat, but Nikki said if he did that she'd report him to the RSPCA. So he did a lot of other tricks. He's quite good. I couldn't see how he was doing them but Greg said he could.

Sita and Karen and Cher did some brilliant singing. I think they're much better than the Spice Girls, and All Saints, and they sing live, they don't just mime to records. We danced while they were singing, or at least some of us did. Liam and Nat, Nikki and Matt, Laura and Bill, even Regina and Bradley. Oh, yeah, and Ollie was dancing with Teraise.

I danced with Joe. I don't fancy him or anything, but it was nice to dance, except that he kept treading on my feet. Ben was dancing with Claire. I don't think there's anything in it. I think he was just missing you.

Anyway, it was a fantastic party, the best I've ever been to. Tina said we might do it again next year. Maybe you'll be able to come.

We took the posters round the town the next morning. They're everywhere, in almost every shop, and we took them to school after the holiday was over. I hate being back at school, don't you?

That's about all I've got to tell you. Mum and Dad send their love and so does Nikki. Ben does, too, and he asked me to write, in capital letters:

WHY HAVEN'T YOU WRITTEN TO HIM?

He said you promised you would. That's all for now.

See you soon.

Lots and lots of love, Emma. XXX

PS. I'll send you one of the posters. They're really good. You could put it on your bedroom wall to remind you of everyone at the Grove.

Alice folded the letter and put it back into the envelope She went upstairs to her bedroom. On top of her dressing table was a box containing the special writing paper her dad had given her on her last birthday.

She took out several sheets, sat at the table and picked up a pen. Her dad was coming to collect her later, but there was plenty of time to write a letter.

She looked down at the paper and started to write.

Dear Ben...

THE END

"Alright," said Emma. She took a deep breath and one final look in her cousin's direction. Alice was staring at the floor. Everyone else was staring at Emma.

"I just want to say," she said, very quietly. Emma wanted to speak loudly and confidently but the words came out as little more than a whisper. She hadn't realised how nervous she felt. She was trembling. Her mouth was dry and the palms of her hands were moist and clammy.

She tried again. "I just want to say..." It was hardly any louder.

"Yeah, we've got that bit," shouted Ollie from the doorway. "But get on with it. What is it you want to say?"

"Ssshh," said Tina. "Give her a chance."

Emma coughed and cleared her throat.

"Come on, Emma, love," called Tina. "We're all listening."

Emma wanted to tell them, she desperately wanted everyone to know the truth. She wanted to shout out: "It wasn't Ben who took the posters, it was Alice. My cousin. Alice is the one who should be banned from the Grove, not Ben." The words were there, ready and waiting to be spoken, but they wouldn't come out.

The sea of faces stared up at her, becoming blurred as she tried to go on. She felt dizzy. Hot. The room was spinning and Emma's legs were like jelly.

"I just want to say," she said for a third time, although it sounded to Emma as though someone else was speaking. Someone far away, in the distance.

And then everything went dark.

• • • • •

"Emma?"

Emma could hear the voice calling, but it was so far away.

"Emma? Can you hear me?"

Of course she could hear. She could hear perfectly well, and the voice was closer now.

"Open your eyes, Emma."

Emma stirred, she didn't want to open her eyes.

"Come on, Emma, wake up. Open your eyes."

Emma's eyelids felt so heavy, she was tired, surely is wasn't time to get up yet. But the voice came again, ordering her to wake up and open her eyes.

Oh, alright, thought Emma. If I have to.

Slowly and reluctantly, Emma opened her eyes. Someone was staring anxiously down at her. It was Tina. She smiled.

"Are you alright, love?" she asked.

Emma didn't know if she was alright. She didn't even know where she was. Or what had happened.

"Just sit up slowly," said Tina. "Let me help."

Tina put one arm under Emma's shoulders and carefully helped her to sit up.

"Here, drink this," said Tina, offering Emma a cup of water.

Emma took the cup and sipped the water. Gradually her eyes began to focus. She was still in the general room. On the stage. Everyone was looking at her. The feeling of confusion was gradually replaced by one of embarrassment.

"You gave us a fright there," said Tina. "You went so pale and then just keeled over. But there's some colour coming back to your cheeks now."

"Is there?" whispered Emma.

"Have you ever fainted before?"

Emma shook her head. "I felt so hot. I couldn't speak."

"Well don't talk too much now. Just sit here and rest. It is hot in here and you were probably a bit nervous about talking to everyone."

Tina turned to the other Grovers. "Right, come on you lot, out you go. The excitement's over."

She glanced over to Alice. "Alice, you look pale as well. You'd better stay in here with Emma."

Alice was pale. She was concerned about her cousin but was also afraid that once Emma had fully recovered she would still tell the Grovers that it was her, and not Ben, who had taken the posters. Part of Alice wanted to go to Emma and comfort her but the other part wanted to stay as far away as possible.

The Grovers began to leave the room but Regina and Laura lingered by the doorway.

"Can we stay?" said Regina to Tina. "She is our friend."

Tina was about to tell Regina and Laura to go out with the other Grovers but she paused and looked at Alice again. She really didn't look very well. Almost worse than Emma.

"Alright," she said to the two waiting girls. "Just sit here quietly with Emma. I've got to phone her mum."

"No, it's alright, you don't have to," said Emma urgently. "I'm fine now."

"I'm sure you are," said Tina with a smile. "But your mum has to know what happened and you ought to go home, just to be on the safe side. Alice too, by the look of her."

She got up and went to the doorway, casting a warning look in Regina and Laura's direction. "Just sit quietly, remember. And keep an eye on Alice as well."

Regina and Laura weren't particularly interested in Alice at that moment. Emma was their friend and she was the one who had fainted.

Alice sat on a chair and watched as Regina and Laura went to the stage and perched on the edge, on either side of Emma. Would it be now? Would Emma tell her two closest friends what she had been unable to tell the whole roomful of Grovers? Regina was bound to ask.

Regina did ask.

"What did you want to say? Was it something terrible? Is that why you fainted?"

"Regina, we're supposed to be sitting here quietly," said Laura.

"It's alright, Laura," said Emma. "I'm fine."

"Well, what was it, then?" asked Regina.

Emma's and Alice's eyes met. Regina's question had given Emma a second opportunity to reveal the truth. She wanted to. She had been so angry when she climbed on to the stage, furious at the way her cousin had let Ben take the blame for her actions. But now the anger had drained away. The stress of the past week and the upset and emotion of the past hour had left her feeling weak and weary. It was too late. Emma just wanted to go home.

But she had to say something, Regina and Laura were waiting for an answer. Emma felt herself blush.

"It was nothing," she said, still looking at Alice. "I was going to thank Regina for all the work she's been doing for the poster competition and the saving energy day. That's all."

"Oh, that was nice," said Laura. "Wasn't it Regina?"

Regina didn't answer. She had spotted the look that passed between Emma and her cousin. It was more than a look. Alice was silently pleading with Emma, begging her not to reveal some guilty secret. Regina just knew it.

Earlier in the day, Emma had suspected that Alice was keeping a secret, and she had stumbled on the truth after spotting her cousin and Ben at the bus stop.

And at that moment, Regina suspected that Emma was keeping a secret. And Regina decided there and then that she would discover the truth.

• • • • •

"There's someone here to see you, Ben."

Ben looked up from the magazine he was reading.

It was the following morning and Ben had been listlessly trying to find ways of filling his time. He couldn't go to the Grove where all his friends were so he had been sitting around at home. Thinking. Mainly about Alice. And Ben wasn't sure how he felt about Alice anymore.

He had wanted to help when he took the blame over the posters because he liked Alice and he sympathised with the tough time she was going through. But that was two days ago and the consequences of his actions were starting to hit. Hard. Ben didn't particularly like being on his own. He missed his mates and, worse than that, he knew that his mates, and everyone else at the Grove, didn't think much of him at the moment.

Yesterday he had waited for Alice and spoken to her at the bus stop. When he offered to go back to the Grove with her so that they could sort things out by telling the truth, Alice had become hesitant and defensive.

She told him that she wasn't sure, she couldn't decide, she didn't think it would work, she needed time to think. Well, that was alright for Alice, but what about him? He was the one who was suffering.

For two days now Ben had been hanging around, waiting for something to happen and keeping his guilty secret from his foster mother, Lou. And he felt bad about that, too.

Ben liked and admired Lou more than anyone else. Lou had been good to Ben, ever since he had come to live at Gallagher's. She had stuck by him through some difficult and painful times. And, in return, Ben had learned to always be straight and honest with Lou. But this time he hadn't been straight. Or honest. He hadn't told her he'd been suspended from the Grove. He didn't want to disappoint Lou.

Now she was standing in the doorway with a slightly puzzled look on her face.

"Who is it?" asked Ben.

Lou turned and looked back into the hallway.

"You'd better come in, love," she said.

It was Alice. As soon as Ben saw her his feelings changed again. She'd done it. She'd gone to the Grove and owned up. She must have done. And now she was here to tell him that everything was fine and the Grovers were waiting for him to return.

But the feeling of elation lasted for only a moment. Ben quickly saw that Alice was looking as miserable and unhappy as ever. She came into the room and waited for Lou to go.

"I'll leave you to it, then," said Lou with a shake of her head. She knew there was something wrong. She'd known ever since Ben had come home two nights earlier. And she knew it had something to do with Alice, the new girl at the Grove, who Ben had mentioned several times during the past week.

But Lou had said nothing, she preferred to wait until her foster children were ready to talk to her about their problems. Ben obviously wasn't ready to talk. Yet. She closed the door, leaving Ben and Alice alone.

Alice sat in the chair opposite Ben.

"Did you go back?" asked Ben.

Alice nodded.

"And did you tell them?"

"I couldn't, Ben," said Alice unhappily. "I wanted to, I really did, but when it came to it, I was too scared. I was frightened. I kept thinking about what my dad would say if he found out. And my mum. They'd be so upset. Everything keeps getting worse and worse."

Ben was rapidly losing his patience. He stood up and began pacing around the room. "But what about me? You'll be going home in a few days. You can forget about the Grove. But I can't. All my mates are there."

"I'm sorry, Ben."

"Is that all you can say?"

"I don't know what else to say."

Ben stopped pacing. He didn't want to argue with Alice. He knew it was difficult for her, too, but she got them both into this mess. He slumped back down into the armchair. "So no-one knows the truth?"

"Emma does. She tried to tell everyone."

"Emma?" said Ben. "How does Emma know?"

"She saw us at the bus stop yesterday and then I told her what really happened, and what you'd done for me. She said she'd split on me if I didn't own up."

"But she didn't."

"She tried, but she fainted."

"She what?"

Ben listened in amazement as Alice told him about the awful few minutes at the Grove the previous evening.

"And what now?" Ben asked when Alice finished. "Where's Emma?"

"At home. Her mum said she had to stay in today. Emma's hardly talking to me."

"I'm not surprised."

"But she told me where you lived when I said I wanted to see you."

"But why, Alice?" said Ben angrily. "Why are you here? What d'you expect me to do? Haven't I done enough? And haven't you got me into enough trouble already?"

"I didn't know what else to do, Ben, or where to go. There's no-one else I can talk to."

Ben stood up. "Yes there is," he said. "You can talk to Lou."

• • • • •

Regina was thinking as she walked. She'd been thinking a lot since yesterday, and for once her thoughts were not concentrated on the *Don't Waste Energy Day*.

She was thinking about Emma. It was obvious that she hadn't told the truth yesterday. She was hiding something. Something important. Something she believed the Grovers should know but was too terrible to tell. It was intriguing. Exciting. But what was it? If only Emma hadn't fainted.

"It had nothing to do with thanking me for all my hard work," muttered Regina as she walked. "Not that they shouldn't thank me."

Regina believed the Grovers had a lot to thank her for. She believed that if it wasn't for her hardly anything would ever get done at the Grove. There was always something for her to do and always something for her to think about.

But now she was thinking about Emma and the secret she was keeping. What could it be? What was Emma going to say? It must have been something awful. The grim possibilities grew and grew in Regina's mind.

She thought hard, like a detective searching for clues. What was the evidence? What had been happening at the Grove recently?

Well, thought Regina, there was the poster competition. But there was nothing wrong with that, except that she should have won, rather than Bradley. Her poster was much better than Bradley's, it was just that the judges had mistakenly thought otherwise. But they had reached their decision fair and square, there was no hint of a fix.

Perhaps it's the saving energy day, thought Regina. But no, it couldn't be that, everything was going to plan.

Then what could it possibly be?

Regina stopped. Ben. Ben had taken the posters and been suspended from the Grove. It had something to do with Ben. Of course. That must be it. It had something to do with Ben. And Alice. Alice was involved somehow, Regina just knew it. She'd seen the way Alice had looked at Emma yesterday. Alice had looked scared. Terrified.

Regina began walking again, but faster. She marched up to Emma's house, pressed the doorbell and waited.

"Oh," said Emma as she opened the door and saw her friend on the doorstep. "It's you."

"How are you?" said Regina with a smile. "Feeling better?"

"There's nothing wrong with me. I just got too hot and felt a bit dizzy, but Mum says I've got to stay in today."

"I thought that was it, when you didn't turn up at the Grove. So I thought I'd come to see you."

Emma smiled. "You'd better come in, then."

Regina followed Emma up to her bedroom. They sat on the beds.

"We can play some CDs if you want," said Emma.

"If you like," said Regina, the detective. "Or we could just talk."

"Talk? What about?"

"I don't know," said Regina innocently. She knew exactly what she wanted to talk about. "Where's Alice?"

"She's gone to..." Emma stopped herself from finishing the sentence. She had been about to say that Alice had gone to see Ben. "She's gone out."

"Where to?" said Regina. "She wasn't at the Grove."

"I... I'm not sure," said Emma. She hated lying. She couldn't do it. It made her blush. Everyone knew when Emma wasn't telling the truth.

Regina knew. "Hasn't gone to see Ben, has she?"

Emma started. "Why d'you say that?"

"Dunno," said Regina. "I just wondered."

"I don't know where she's gone," said Emma hurriedly. "She went out. Maybe she's gone into town."

"Mmm," said Regina. She went to Emma's collection of tapes and CDs stacked on the dressing table and casually glanced at some of the covers.

"What was it you were going to say yesterday, Emma?" she said without looking back. "Before you fainted?"

"I told you what it was," said Emma, trying to appear calm. "I was just going to thank you."

Regina turned to face her friend. "Emma, that's not true, is it?"

Emma didn't reply.

"I'm you're friend, Emma," said Regina, "and I know there's something wrong. It's got something to do with Ben, hasn't it? And Alice."

"Regina, stop it!" snapped Emma. "Stop asking me these questions. I can't tell you anything. I can't!"

• • • • •

"Well, Alice, you've certainly been having quite a time of it lately. And I don't mean just this week."

Alice sank back against the deep, soft cushions on the old sofa. It had been good to talk to Lou. She felt much better.

She had been hesitant at first, but Lou had been so nice, so kind and so understanding, that soon Alice had found herself saying all the things she had wanted to say for months.

She told Lou everything, the whole painful story. How her dad had left and gone to live with his new girlfriend. How hurt and confused she felt. How neither her dad nor mum would talk to her about it because her dad was too embarrassed and her mum was too upset. She just wanted to know, she said, and to understand.

But no-one would talk, no-one would explain. And when she tried to talk they said things like 'It'll get better in time' or 'These things happen' or 'You'll understand when you're older'. But it wasn't getting better. It hurt just as much and she still didn't understand.

Then Alice told Lou what had happened at the Grove. For days she'd watched the Grovers enjoying themselves, laughing, smiling, joking. It made her feel worse and worse until finally she just wanted to stop them smiling. She wanted them to feel as bad as she did.

That was why she tore the posters from the walls. That was why she'd been so horrible to her cousin, and to Ben. That was why she let Ben take the blame for what she had done.

Lou just listened. She nodded and sighed and smiled, but only spoke when she felt that Alice needed a little encouragement to continue with her story. It was a familiar story, one that Lou had heard many times before.

She smiled kindly. "You know, Alice," she said, "I've had lots of youngsters stay with me over the years, some of them with stories like yours, some of them with much more difficult and painful stories." She looked across to where Ben was sitting. "Eh, Ben?"

Ben nodded.

"But the point is, Alice," Lou continued, "they were all feeling hurt and confused and vulnerable when they first arrived, just like you are. They all needed someone to talk to, someone to listen, someone to understand and someone to tell them that lots of other youngsters have felt exactly the way they are feeling."

"I know," said Alice, "but why did it have to happen to me?"

"I can't answer that," said Lou with a shake of her head. "But it has happened. You're going to have to accept it and look at the positive things that you've got."

"Like what?"

"Well, your mum and dad are both still around, a lot of youngsters don't have that. And I'm sure they both love you."

"Sometimes it feels as though my dad doesn't. Sometimes when I see him at the weekend it's almost like he's counting off the minutes until he can take me home."

"Perhaps he's confused, too. This is all new for him as well, remember."

"But he left us," said Alice sharply.

"Yes, he did, but that doesn't mean he's not confused. Everyone is. Your mum, your dad, even your dad's new girlfriend. Everyone's feeling a bit confused and vulnerable. Just like you. But you're the only one who's been brave enough to say it."

"I'm not brave," said Alice.

"Yes you are," replied Lou. "It takes courage to own up to how you're really feeling. To admit how frightened you are. Maybe your mum and dad need you to help them to admit how they're feeling."

"But I couldn't even own up to what I'd done at the Grove. I was too scared."

"But you can still put that right, can't you?"

"Can I?" said Alice hesitantly.

"Go back to the Grove, Alice," said Lou. "Go back now, with Ben."

"I don't know if I can."

Lou smiled. "But I know you can. Go back and tell them you're sorry for what you did."

"They might not give me another chance."

"No, maybe not, but you won't find out unless you try. And you'll feel a lot better for trying, Alice."

Alice looked into Lou's warm, smiling, friendly eyes. If only everyone was like Lou, she thought, then everything would be so easy.

She turned to Ben. "Will you come with me?"

"Yeah," said Ben. "Of course I will."

Alice stood up. "Alright," she said. "I'll try."

• • • • •

Regina was on her way back to the Grove. Emma had refused to answer any more questions and when Regina persisted they came close to having a row.

So Regina stopped asking questions. It didn't matter anyway. Emma's reluctance to talk merely confirmed Regina's suspicions. Her friend was keeping a dark secret concerning Ben and Alice. All Regina needed to do now was to work out exactly what that secret was. She would have to speak to some of the other members of the Grove.

She hurried up the drive, dashed through the main door and walked straight into her cousin, Teraise.

"Regina!" said Teraise grumpily. "Why don't you look where you're going?" She went to walk away.

"Teraise, wait a minute," said Regina quickly. "There's something I want to ask you."

"Well, hurry up," said Teraise, pausing in the corridor. Teraise was fond of her young cousin and she liked having her around at home, most of the time. But when she was at the Grove, Teraise preferred the company of friends of her own age.

"You know, yesterday," said Regina, "when Emma got up on the stage to say something?"

"Yeah."

"What d'you think she was going to say?"

Teraise looked blankly at her cousin. "Regina, how should I know? And what does it matter now, anyway?"

"It was something important," said Regina. "And it was something to do with Ben. And Alice."

Teraise suddenly looked interested. "How do you know?" she asked.

"I know," said Regina mysteriously. "Listen."

Teraise did listen. Closely. Intently. And by the time Regina had finished outlining her suspicions, Teraise, too, was suspicious. "What is it, though?" she said. "Ben took the posters, maybe it's got something to do with that."

"Yeah," said Regina. "I'd already thought of the posters."

"I'll go and ask Claire and Nat," said Teraise. "See what they think."

"Good idea," said Regina. "Let me know what they say."

Teraise was about to go off in search of her friends when Bradley appeared in the corridor. He was smiling.

"Oh, Teraise," he said. "Could I ask you something?"

"What is it?" said Teraise. Being questioned by younger members of Byker Grove was becoming a habit.

"Well, you know I'm a magician?"

"I had heard."

"Well, I've decided to do this famous old trick at the party on Friday."

"So what?"

"I need a glamorous female assistant to help me."

"Are you winding me up, because if you are..."

"No, I'm not. Honest."

"What is this trick?"

"It's called 'Sawing The Lady In Half', but it's perfectly safe. I won't really saw you in half, it's what's known as an optical illus..."

"Stop!"

Bradley stopped.

"You're quite right, Bradley," said Teraise. "You won't be sawing me in half. I wouldn't come anywhere near you and a saw."

Teraise walked away.

Bradley sighed and turned to Regina. "I don't suppose you..."

"Don't be silly, Bradley," said Regina dismissively. "But listen, I've got something to tell you."

Bradley listened as Regina repeated the story she had told Teraise, and at the same time, in the games room, Teraise was telling the story to Nat and Claire.

And so it continued. In less than an hour, everyone at the Grove had heard the story. Nat told Liam, Bradley told Barry, Liam told Ollie, Barry told Joe, Ollie told Karen, Joe told Bill, Karen told Cher, and so on, and so on.

Each time the story was told it changed a little, it was exaggerated and embellished – some of the Grovers had more vivid imaginations than others. The Grove was buzzing with excitement and speculation. Everyone had an opinion, everyone thought they knew the answer to the great Ben and Alice poster mystery.

The most popular theory was that Alice had made Ben take the posters as a test, before she would agree to go out with him. But there were other guesses, some of which might have been possible, but most were completely impossible.

But no-one guessed what had really happened.

Eventually even Tina heard the story. She was in the office when Cher came in to tell her the exciting news. But Tina didn't find the news exciting, she found it worrying. Tina didn't approve of gossip and rumour going around the Grove, it almost always ended in someone being hurt. But there was even more to worry about. What if there was some truth in the rumour?

"Where does this come from?" she asked. "Who started this story?"

"I don't know," said Cher. "It might have been Liam, or Nat. Or maybe it was Ollie. I don't really know, but everyone's talking about it."

Everyone was talking about it, the story was sensational, true or false. But the truth was about to be revealed. Ben and Alice were walking up the drive.

Stumpy saw them first. He'd heard the story from Bill and gone looking for someone else to tell. But by then everyone knew so Stumpy told Wombat, and then decided to take his dog for a run in the grounds. But as soon as he stepped out through the doorway he saw Ben and Alice approaching.

Stumpy's eyes bulged. This time he'd be first with the news. He turned around, shouted to Wombat to follow him, and went hurtling into the crowded general room.

"They're coming!" he shouted at the top of his voice.

"Who are?" said Regina, breaking off from her conversation with Laura.

"Ben and Alice!" shouted Stumpy. "I saw them first! They're coming up the drive!"

"I knew it," whispered Regina.

Tina had also heard Stumpy's shout. She stepped out of the office just as Ben and Alice came in through the main doors, completely unaware of what had been going on at the Grove during the past hour.

"Ben…"

"I know I'm suspended, Tina," said Ben before Tina could finish. "But Alice has got something to say. It involves me, too, and what happened with the posters."

Tina nodded. "Oh, dear," she said quietly as she followed Ben and Alice into the general room.

The noise and chatter of the room was immediately hushed. Alice and Ben stood at the front of the stage and waited as more Grovers hurried in from other rooms and filled every available space.

Everyone was there. Everyone but Emma, thought Alice, as she remembered the previous day. She was finally about to do exactly as Emma had demanded but Emma wasn't there to witness it. Alice couldn't help smiling at the irony of the situation.

Regina was watching Alice closely. "She's smiling," she whispered to Laura. "She thinks this is funny. What a cheek!"

Alice was ready. "There's something I've got to say," she said. "Emma wanted to tell you this yesterday, before she fainted."

"I told you," whispered Regina to Laura.

"It's about the posters, and what really happened."

"I told…"

"Be quiet," said Laura before Regina could tell her again that she had told her.

Regina was quiet. The general room was absolutely silent.

Alice took a deep breath. "Ben didn't take the posters," she said. "It was me."

Many of the Grovers gasped, others gazed in confusion at each other and still more stared at Alice in total disbelief. They'd all known that the great poster mystery had something to do with Alice. But not this. This was impossible.

"But we saw Ben," said Karen. "He had the posters in his hands."

"Yeah, we caught him red-handed," added Nat. "Are you trying to tell us we didn't see him?"

"Ben wasn't taking the posters," said Alice. "He was bringing them back. He saw me take them, earlier. I took them up to the attic and hid them. Ben followed me – I didn't even know he was there. And when I ran out, Ben got the posters and tried to put them back. But you saw him before he could do it."

"Is this true, Ben?" said Tina.

"Yeah, it's true," said Ben quietly.

"But why didn't you say something when you had the chance? You could have told us the truth."

"He was trying to save me," said Alice.

"Ah," whispered Karen to Cher. "Isn't that romantic?"

Nat overheard Karen's comment. "Stupid if you ask me," she said.

"No-one was asking you," said Karen.

"I want to tell you all that I'm very sorry," said Alice loudly. "I'm sorry for taking the posters. I've never done anything like that before. I was upset, but it was a stupid and horrible thing to do. And

I'm sorry for what I did to Ben, I should never have let him take the blame for me. And even though she's not here today, I want you to know that I'm sorry for how I've been to Emma. And to all of you, too. I'm really sorry."

Alice's voice trailed off. She waited, expecting someone to tell her to get out and never come back. But no-one did. They were too shocked. Too stunned.

Ben was the first to speak.

"Am I still suspended, Tina?" he asked.

"Of course not," Tina replied.

"Then I want to say that I reckon we should give Alice another chance. You can see she's sorry for what she did. She's apologised and there's no real harm done, so let's just forget it."

No-one answered, so Ben tried again. "Can't we give her another chance? Please?"

YOU CHOOSE DO THE GROVERS GIVE ALICE ANOTHER CHANCE?

YES GO TO THE NEXT PAGE

NO GO TO PAGE 176

"No!" Regina spoke up loudly and firmly. She was the first to answer Ben's question but many more of the Grovers were thinking exactly the same thing. "She took the posters, she lied, she almost ruined everything. She should be suspended, like Ben was!"

"It's not up to you, Regina," said Nikki. "And anyway, Alice has apologised. She knows what she did was wrong."

"Apologising doesn't make it alright," said Nat. "I reckon she should be banned completely."

"Well, I don't," said Laura.

Regina turned to her friend and glared.

"Well, I don't, Regina, so there," shouted Laura.

Other Grovers began to voice their opinions and several arguments started to break out. Tina could see that the situation was rapidly getting out of hand.

"Quiet!" she shouted, but the arguments continued. Tina shouted again, even louder than before. "Quiet, the lot of you!"

Tina paused. She knew about Alice's problems at home, Emma had told her when she first asked about Alice's temporary membership of the Grove. Tina wondered now if, perhaps, she should have kept a closer eye on Alice during the past week.

She had listened carefully to everything Alice said. It had taken a great deal of courage to stand in front of the Grovers and apologise. Alice hadn't tried to make excuses for her behaviour, she had simply admitted everything and said that she was sorry. She hadn't even asked to be given another chance, Ben had done that.

Tina wanted to give Alice another chance, but she knew that it would be pointless unless all the Grovers agreed with her decision. Any lingering resentment towards Alice would quickly spread and Alice's second week at the Grove might easily be even more miserable than the first.

Tina needed the Grovers to be on her side. There had to be a way. And there was. Tina suddenly realised that the best way of getting the decision she wanted would be by letting the Grovers make the decision themselves. Or at least by letting the Grovers think they had made the decision themselves.

"There's obviously a lot of strong feeling about this," she said quietly. "And I think the fairest thing to do would be for you all to decide on whether or not Alice remains a member of the Grove. We'll take a vote on it."

There was a murmur of excitement as the Grovers quickly tried to work out who would vote in favour and who would be against Alice staying on.

"But before we take the vote, there are one or two things I want to say."

Liam turned to Ollie. "Here we go," he said.

"What d'you mean?" said Ollie.

"Tactics. She's got it all worked out."

"What?"

"You wait and see."

And Tina did have it all worked out. She stood between Alice and Ben, and addressed the Grovers. "First of all, I've got to say that what Alice did was very wrong, and you can all, just by looking at her, see that she has suffered for what she did."

The Grovers stared at Alice. It was true. She looked pale and tired. She had suffered.

"For two days," Tina continued, "Alice has known that she did wrong, not once, but twice. She took the posters and then she let Ben take the blame. Imagine the guilt she felt. Imagine what it must have been like."

The Grovers looked at Alice again. They tried to imagine. It must have been awful.

"But why did she do it?" said Tina dramatically. "What made Alice act in this silly and irresponsible way? She's already told us that she's never done anything like this before, so what was it?"

Once more, the Grovers glanced in Alice's direction. What was it? What could have driven her to do such a reckless thing?

"Let's consider the facts," said Tina, sounding more and more like a barrister in a court case. "Firstly, it's no secret, and most of you know, that Alice has had problems at home. Her mum and dad split up recently. Now I know that some of you can sympathise with her in that. Some of you have been through similar experiences and you know the upset and stress it can cause. And I'm sure you can all understand how difficult and painful it must have been for Alice."

"Brings tears to your eyes, doesn't it?" whispered Liam to Ollie.

"Ssshh," said Ollie. He was listening intently to Tina.

"Secondly," said Tina, "Alice was new to the Grove. She was a stranger here. She saw you enjoying yourselves, getting excited about the poster competition and the party while all the time she was feeling lonely and uncertain about the future."

She paused to look closely at all of the Grovers. They were captivated by her story. One or two really did have tears in their eyes.

Tina's voice became quieter and quieter. "Alice felt lower and sadder as the week went by, until finally…" Tina's voice had almost faded away to nothing. She paused. One second, two seconds, three seconds, and then shouted: "…she snapped!"

Every one of the Grovers jumped. Regina almost fell off her chair.

"She snapped and she took the posters," said Tina. "She didn't want to destroy them. She just hid them. It was silly and reckless, but can any of us say that we've never done anything that was silly and reckless. And can we really blame Alice? After everything she's been through recently?"

This time the Grovers looked at each other. No-one spoke, but they were all thinking the same thing. Poor Alice. How she's suffered. How could they possibly blame her?

"I think we should take the vote now," said Tina, "but there's just one thing more I want to say before we do."

The Grovers listened again.

"Regina has been telling us for some time how important it is not to waste energy and Regina is absolutely right."

Regina beamed.

Tina was reaching the end of her speech. "But isn't it a waste of our own energy if we bear grudges? Shouldn't we all spread positive energy by learning to forgive and forget. Grovers, the decision is yours."

"What a performance," said Liam. He was tempted to burst into a round of applause.

"Those who think that Alice should be forgiven and allowed to stay on as a member of the Grove, please put your hands up now," said Tina.

The hands began to go up. First the 'certainties' – those who had already believed that Alice should be given a second chance, then the 'not sures' who had been convinced by Tina's speech, and finally the 'definitely nots', those Grovers who, a few minutes earlier, had been firmly convinced that Alice should never again be allowed to step foot in the Grove.

Nat was last but one, but her hand went up when she saw that Claire's and Teraise's hands were already pointing at the ceiling.

Last of all was Regina. She was surrounded by her friends, Laura, Barry, Bradley, Bill, Joe and Stumpy. They all had their hands up and Stumpy was even holding up one of Wombat's paws with his free hand.

Regina raised her arm slowly.

Tina smiled. "Then it's unanimous," she said. "Grovers, I'm proud of you."

The Grovers seemed proud of themselves, too. They were delighted to have made the right decision and they congratulated themselves by bursting into a round of applause.

Alice just stared, she was shocked and bewildered. In just a few minutes she had gone from being the least popular person at the Grove to everyone's favourite.

She walked, almost in a daze, to where Tina was standing. "Thanks, Tina," she said. "I can't believe it."

"Nothing to do with me," said Tina with a smile. "They decided, not me."

Alice returned the smile. "No," she said, "it had nothing at all to do with you."

"Now you can enjoy the rest of your time at the Grove."

"I will," said Alice. "I've got to go back and tell Emma what's happened. She won't believe it, either. But I will be back. Tomorrow."

Tina returned to the office, highly satisfied at what she had managed to achieve, and a few minutes later Liam poked his head around the door.

"You're wasted here," he said.

"What d'you mean?" said Tina.

"You should be a judge."

Tina smiled.

"No, not a judge," said Liam. "You should be Prime Minister."

• • • • •

Alice was right. Emma didn't believe it. Not at first. It took Alice a long time, but she finally convinced her cousin that it was all perfectly, happily true. Emma was delighted, but she was also disappointed that she hadn't been at the Grove to witness the incredible scene. She insisted that Alice gave her a full account of everything that had happened, not leaving out one single detail.

So Alice told her and, gradually, as the story unfolded, the two girls found themselves growing closer again. Soon, they were good friends again, just as they always had been.

"Even Regina?" Emma asked excitedly, after Alice told her that all the Grovers voted in favour of her staying on at the Grove.

"Even Regina," said Alice. "Eventually. Everyone wanted to give me another chance, every single person. And then, when I was leaving, Regina came over and told me she was glad I was staying. She wants us to be friends."

"Brilliant," said Emma. "Well, I'm definitely not staying at home tomorrow. I'm coming to the Grove with you." She smiled at her cousin. "Oh, Alice, I'm so pleased you went back, and I'm so pleased everything's sorted out."

"Not quite everything," Alice replied. "There's something else I've got to do."

"Is there?"

Alice nodded. "I've got to tell your mum."

"Have you?"

"It's only fair. I've got to tell her everything."

"Oh, dear," said Emma.

It wasn't easy. Emma's mum was shocked to hear all that had happened to her niece during her week at the Grove. But Alice left nothing out. She was as honest with her aunt as she had been with Lou earlier in the day.

And just like Lou, Emma's mum listened without interrupting. Her face was grave and concerned at the beginning, but it gradually brightened, and by the time Alice finished her story, Emma's mum could see that her niece was looking and feeling almost like her old self.

"I'm sorry, Auntie Jackie," said Alice finally. "I've been awful this week, but I'll be better now, I promise."

"I'm just glad to see you smiling again, pet," said her aunt. "But why didn't you talk to me? Why didn't you tell me how bad you were feeling?"

Alice shook her head. "I don't know. I wanted to. I've been wanting to talk about it for ages."

Emma's mum smiled. "D'you know, you're a lot more like your dad than I realised."

That night, after Emma and Alice had gone to bed, Emma's mum made a telephone call to her brother, Alice's dad.

And it was a long conversation.

• • • • •

Alice's second week at the Grove was completely different from the first. She was happy, and she enjoyed every moment. She spent time with Ben and with her cousin Emma, and also got to know some of the older Grovers.

But Alice never neglected Regina. In fact, she was particularly nice to Regina. No task was too difficult and no little job was too much trouble. Alice had a lot of making up to do, and she did it, and in return Regina came to consider that Alice was a special friend of hers.

They sat down together and wrote out a list of everything that would be needed for the party, and they then went off to the supermarket together and returned carrying bulging plastic bags full of food and drink.

Meanwhile, the grounds of the Grove were being transformed. The huge bonfire was built from pieces of scrap wood and old boxes, a barbecue, tables and benches were set up, and a temporary stage made of wooden planks and crates stood ready for the entertainment.

Last-minute rehearsals took place behind closed doors. Karen, Sita and Cher banned everyone else from going anywhere near the television room where they rehearsed their songs.

Bradley retired to the attic to practise his magic. He had reluctantly accepted that he was never going to find someone willing to be sawn in half, even if it wasn't for real, so he had returned to some of his old magic tricks. And when he was completely satisfied that his tricks were perfect, he invited a few of his closest friends up to the attic to watch a final, dress rehearsal. They emerged impressed.

Don't Waste Energy Day dawned bright and dry. But cold. "Don't worry," Regina said to Alice, "it won't rain, I watched the weather forecast on telly last night."

Regina had arrived early, and so had Alice, at Regina's special invitation. They walked around the Grove together. Regina was carrying a clipboard with her list of rules and regulations for *Don't Waste Energy Day* pinned on to it.

"I'll read them out as we go," said Regina. They went from room to room, ensuring that no more than one light was switched on in any room and that all the radiators were turned down to half their previous settings.

Doors were closed, taps were turned firmly off and the drinks machine and television were switched off, with notices fixed to them stating that they were not to be used for the whole day.

By the time the other Grovers began to arrive, the building was in semi-darkness and looking distinctly gloomy. And it was cold.

"It's too cold," complained Bradley. "My hands are freezing, and a magician mustn't have cold hands. I won't be able to do my tricks properly."

"Put some gloves on, then," Regina told him. "And don't moan."

More of the Grovers moaned during the day but Regina was quick to remind them that they were making an important point for the whole of Newcastle to see.

"We take all these things for granted," she said. "Gas, electricity, hot running water. Just imagine what it would be like if we didn't have them."

"But we have got them," said Bradley. "And my hands are cold."

"It'll be worth it, Bradley," Regina replied. "Don't forget we're gonna be in the *Byker Post*."

Midway through the afternoon, the photographer from the *Byker Post* arrived, bringing with him a large, wrapped package.

"It's the posters," yelled Regina as the package was carried into the general room and placed on the stage. "Open it, quickly."

Tina produced a pair of scissors and the Grovers crowded round as she cut the cord tied around the package and pulled out the top poster. The shiny poster looked even better than Bradley's original work. The huge, yellow face smiled even brighter, the deep blue eyes were more brilliant, and underneath, the shimmering red lettering stood out and almost shouted: 'Be Happy – Save Energy.'

"Brilliant," said Bradley. "Even though I say it myself."

Alice studied the poster. Bradley's original version was the first one she had ripped from the wall a week earlier. She had hated it so much then. How things had changed in just a week. She looked at the happy, smiling face and realised that she was smiling, too.

"We'll all be taking them round the town tomorrow," said Regina. "But we'll put one up in here for now."

"Regina?" It was Alice.

"Yes?" said Regina.

"Can I do it?"

Regina smiled. "Of course you can, Alice."

Alice took the poster and fixed it to the wall. She turned to Bradley. "You're right, Bradley," she said. "It's brilliant."

Bradley smiled and rubbed his hands together. Suddenly, they didn't feel cold at all.

"Right," said the photographer from the *Byker Post* as the Grovers admired Bradley's art work. "Let's get this photo taken, shall we? We'll do it outside. Bring one of the posters."

He led the Grovers out to the front of the building. "We'll have the artist and young Regina crouching down on the step with one other person. They can hold the poster between them."

The photographer glanced around at the other Grovers. "Perhaps you'd like to join them?"

He was looking at Alice.

"Me?" said Alice. "But..."

"Oh yes, come on, Alice," said Regina. "You've worked really hard this week."

Alice looked at Tina. She wasn't sure.

"Go on," said Tina. "You're a member of Byker Grove, aren't you?"

Alice nodded and joined Regina and Bradley on the step.

"Now the rest of you just gather round them," said the photographer. "Close as you can, but make sure we can see all your faces. And let me see you smile."

Karen, Cher and Sita were first to get into position. They made sure they were in the centre of the picture by standing directly behind Regina, Bradley and Alice.

"Told you they'd need a bit of glamour," said Karen to Nat, who'd been one of the last to join the group and was standing at one side. She scowled.

"I said smile," said the photographer, noticing Nat's fierce look. Nat smiled.

The Grovers huddled together and the photographer looked into his camera. He adjusted the lens on the front and was about to take the photograph when he stopped, looked up and turned to Tina who was standing at his side.

"What's that dog doing there?"

"Oh, that's Wombat," laughed Tina. "He's got to be in the photo. He's a member of Byker Grove, too."

The photographer shrugged. "Fair enough," he said, looking into the camera again. "Right, hold the poster up. That's it. Keep still everyone and say chee… No, don't say cheese, say 'Be Happy'."

"Be Happy!" yelled the Grovers and the camera clicked.

• • • • •

Bradley had a new name. When he'd first started his clowning and magic act he'd called himself Mr Jolly Wally. But Bradley had decided that his new, more sophisticated act deserved a new, more sophisticated name. So Mr Jolly Wally was now 'The Magnificent Bradley'.

The Magnificent Bradley was midway through his performance at the party and most of the Grovers sat on benches, watching.

The party was going well, almost as perfectly as The Magnificent Bradley's tricks.

The huge bonfire had illuminated the dark night. It had blazed for more than an hour and was beginning to die down. Now the grounds of Byker Grove were bathed in a more gentle light. Candles burned in jars on the tables, and lamps with more candles hung from some of the closest trees.

Ollie and Liam had amazed the Grovers by offering to be barbecue chefs. And apart from a few blackened sausages and burnt burgers, the food had been delicious.

The Magnificent Bradley was reaching the climax of his act. Sadly for Bradley there was no sawing involved, but as his magician's cloak swirled around, he put both hands up to his mouth and appeared to pull out a long string of coloured handkerchiefs. The Grovers clapped and cheered as Bradley took a slow and extravagant bow.

"Get off!" yelled Liam with a grin, but even he was secretly impressed.

Bradley swept off the stage and Regina swept on to it.

"Thank you, The Magnificent Bradley," she said. "And now, it's time for our top of the bill act. Let's give a real Byker Grove welcome to Karen, Sita and Cher!"

The Grovers burst into applause as the three girls ran on to the stage. They were wearing matching dresses in blue, yellow and red, the same colours as on Bradley's poster.

The girls began to sing, and as their sweet harmonies filled the evening air, the grounds of Byker Grove were bathed in firelight and candlelight. Everyone watched and listened in absolute silence as the shadows cast by the bonfire flickered across the stage. At the end of the song every one of the Grovers stood and applauded loudly.

"Thanks very much," said Karen. "We're going to do a slow one now, so if any of you lads fancy asking someone to dance, now's your chance."

Ben was the first to move. He went to Alice. "D'you want to dance?" Alice nodded and they walked to the space in front of the stage. Ben put his arms around Alice's waist, she put hers around his shoulders and they danced slowly to the rhythm of the song.

Liam strode up to Nat. "D'you wanna have a go?"

"Oh, Liam, you've got such a way with words," laughed Nat. "How could I refuse?"

Ollie wasn't going to be left out. He sidled sheepishly over to Claire and asked her to dance. Claire nodded and got up. Bill was next. He asked Laura if she would dance. Laura blushed, but walked with him into the dancing area. Gradually more and more of the Grovers began to dance.

Regina walked over to where Bradley was sitting. "Do you want to dance?"

"I thought we were supposed to do the asking?" said Bradley.

"I can't wait all night," said Regina. "D'you want to or not?"

Bradley shrugged, nodded and got up to dance with Regina.

Tina watched from the side of the stage. "Ah," she whispered. "It's so romantic."

Ben and Alice were dancing closely.

"What time tomorrow are you going home?" asked Ben.

"In the evening. My dad said he'll come at about seven."

"I'll miss you," said Ben.

"And I'll miss you," replied Alice. "But I'll write to you. And I'll see you again. And we've got tomorrow. I want to help with getting the posters put up."

"Yeah," said Ben. "We've got tomorrow."

"I've had a fantastic time, Ben," said Alice. "Thanks to you."

The song ended and Ben and Alice kissed.

• • • • •

No-one worked harder than Alice the next day. Regina had gathered the Grovers together in the general room that morning and told them there were five hundred posters to distribute.

"The party was last night," she said. "Now we've got to get down to work. Take as many posters as you want and let's see how many we can get put up by five o'clock," she said.

Alice seemed to want to distribute most of the posters herself. She was determined to do everything she could to make up for her actions of more than a week ago, so she and Ben carried away great armfuls of posters.

"We'll never get rid of all these," Ben said.

"Yes we will," said Alice confidently.

The Grovers set off in every direction and soon posters began to appear in shop windows all over Newcastle.

Ben and Alice hardly stopped working. They bought drinks and sandwiches at lunchtime but when Ben suggested they sit down for a while Alice told him that there wasn't time to sit down and that they could eat and drink perfectly well as they went along.

By mid-afternoon most of the posters were gone.

"We should have brought more," said Alice to Ben as they walked out of a shoe shop, having talked the manager into putting a poster in the front window.

"I think we've done our bit," Ben replied. "We took more posters than anyone else."

"Yeah, I suppose so," said Alice. "But we've got to get rid of these last few."

"We'll be running out of shops at this rate," said Ben. "We don't have to go in every shop in Newcastle. We can leave some for the others."

Alice smiled. "I just want to do what I can."

"Yeah, I know."

"Right, let's try the shop next door," said Alice.

The last few posters took longer to place, mainly because most of the shops already had them. But they did it. Alice refused to give up. And by late afternoon, they had all gone.

They caught the bus back to the Grove, they were too weary to walk. Alice felt tired, but very happy.

They got off the bus and trudged up the drive. Alice was looking at the building as they walked.

"My last time," she said.

Ben looked at her. "I know," he said. "I was thinking that, too."

They went into the crowded general room. Everyone else seemed to have finished before Alice and Ben, even Regina.

"We wondered when you'd get back," said Emma.

"We wanted to get all the posters put up," said Alice.

"You've done more than anyone else," said Regina. "Thanks."

"We enjoyed it," said Alice. "Didn't we, Ben?"

"Yeah," said Ben. "Sort of."

Tina came into the room.

"Ben," she called from the doorway. "Can I have a word? In the office?"

"Yeah," said Ben. He looked puzzled. "Not in trouble again, am I?"

"No, you're not in trouble," said Tina with a laugh, as Ben followed her out of the room.

It was past five o'clock and Alice knew that she would soon have to leave the Grove for the final time. Her dad would be at Emma's house in less than two hours, and she still had to pack and get ready to go home.

"We'd better go soon," she said quietly to Emma.

"Yeah," said Emma. "We'll go now if you like."

Alice sighed and nodded. She had been feeling so happy just a few minutes earlier, but she suddenly felt sad. She gazed around the general room. So much had happened at Byker Grove during the past two weeks. She would never forget it. Alice was about to start saying goodbye to her friends when a voice called from the doorway.

"Alice!"

Tina was back. With Ben. And in Ben's hands was a rolled up poster. He walked to Alice and handed it to her.

"We wanted you to have this," he said. "To remind you of Byker Grove. And us."

"I thought I'd seen the last one of these," said Alice as she unravelled the poster.

"Yeah, but that one's different."

And it was. Every member of Byker Grove had signed the poster and written a message. Even Wombat had left a paw print.

Ben's message and signature was under the smiling face, in the centre of the poster. He had written: 'Keep smiling, Alice, and be happy. See you soon. With love, Ben.'

• • • • •

Alice and her dad were driving home. It was dark outside, and as Alice stared out through the window, she was thinking of the friends she had grown to know and like so much during her holiday.

Her dad had arrived at Emma's right on time. Alice had finished packing and was sitting in the kitchen, anxiously looking at the clock, when the back door opened and her dad walked in.

"Dad," said Alice happily as they hugged, "I'm really glad to see you."

"And I'm really glad to see you, love," said her dad. "I've missed you."

Emma's mum made a pot of tea and then they sat at the table and Alice's dad listened as Alice and Emma told him all the good things that had happened during the week. Just the good things. Alice had decided that she would tell her dad, and her mum, the bad things too, but they could wait.

Then there had been tears as Alice said goodbye to her cousin and her aunt and uncle.

And now they were on their way home. "You know, Alice," said Alice's dad. "I've been thinking a lot while you've been away."

"Have you, Dad?" said Alice.

"Yeah, and I think it's time we had a proper talk."

"What about?"

"About everything. We haven't talked properly since… since I left, and we should have done. It's my fault, I've never been very good at talking. But I've spoken to your mum, too, and she agrees. We all need to talk."

"Oh," said Alice.

"What d'you think, then?"

"I think it's great, Dad. I'm glad."

They drove in silence for a few minutes.

"Was this your idea, Dad?" said Alice eventually.

Her dad hesitated. "Well, sort of," he said. "But your Auntie Jackie mentioned it, too."

Alice smiled. "Good old Auntie Jackie," she said.

THE END

"No!" Regina spoke up loudly and firmly. She was the first to answer Ben's question but many more of the Grovers were thinking exactly the same thing. "She took the posters, she lied, she almost ruined everything. She should be suspended, like Ben was!"

"It's not up to you, Regina," said Nikki. "And anyway, Alice has apologised. She knows what she did was wrong."

"Apologising doesn't make it alright," said Nat. "I reckon she should be banned completely."

"Yeah, so do I," said Regina.

"Well, I don't," said Laura.

Regina turned to her friend and scowled.

"Well, I don't, Regina, so there," shouted Laura.

The noise in the general room began to rise and so did the temperature. Several arguments were developing and Tina could see that the situation was rapidly getting out of hand.

"Quiet!" she shouted, but the rows continued. Tina shouted again, even louder than before. "Quiet, the lot of you!"

The room went quiet and the arguing Grovers had to be content with glaring at each other. "Nikki's quite right, Regina," said Tina. "Whether or not Alice is allowed to stay at the Grove isn't up to you. It isn't up to any of you. It's my decision."

"But I think..."

"Thank you, Regina," said Tina. "We know what you think." She turned to Ben and Alice. "I'd like you two to come into the office with me."

Ben and Alice followed Tina to the office and as soon as the door had closed the rowing in the general room began again.

"Look, Alice has been going through a terrible time lately," said Nikki. "Her mum and dad split up and her dad's got a new girlfriend."

"So what's so unusual in that?" said Karen.

"Well, some of us here might just understand how bad she's been feeling."

"What if we do?" said Teraise. "Doesn't mean to say she can go around spoiling things for other people."

"You just have to get on with it," said Nat. "Don't expect me to feel sorry for her."

"We wouldn't expect you to feel sorry for anyone," said Cher.

"Well, that's what she wants," said Nat angrily. "Just trying to get attention."

"Perhaps she is," said Sita, "but there's a reason for it. We ought to be sympathetic."

"Why?" said Ollie. "If you're gonna do something wrong you've got to be prepared to accept the consequences."

"Oh, that's good coming from you," said Karen.

"But what's the point in us punishing Alice when she's already going through a bad time," Sita continued. "I think we should give her another chance."

"I agree," said Karen.

"You would," said Nat.

The argument raged backwards and forwards between the older members of the Grove. The junior Grovers mainly sat and watched and nodded or shook their heads. Apart from Regina, of course.

"I think we should take a vote on it," she declared.

"On what?" said Nat irritably.

"We should vote on whether or not she stays here."

"Look, Regina," said Sita. "Tina's already told you that it's her decision, not ours."

"I know," said Regina indignantly. "But we can say what we think. We're the members of Byker Grove. It's our club."

The room was suddenly silent again, as the Grovers considered Regina's suggestion.

"Perhaps she's right," said Sita. "Perhaps we should let Tina know what the majority of us think."

"Yeah," said Karen. "Let's take a vote on it. It might help Tina with her decision."

Tina had already made her decision. She had watched and listened very carefully as Alice apologised to the Grovers. And she had been impressed by Alice's courage and honesty. Alice hadn't made excuses for her behaviour, she had simply admitted everything and said that she was sorry. She hadn't even asked to be given another chance, Ben had done that.

Tina wanted to give Alice another chance. She knew about her problems at home, Emma had told her when she first asked about Alice's temporary membership of the Grove. Tina wondered now if perhaps she should have kept a closer eye on Alice during the past week.

But Tina also knew that having previously suspended Ben, she could hardly let Alice off with no punishment at all. She was a member of the Grove and she had to stick to the rules, just like everyone else.

Tina had made up her mind, but she wanted to be as gentle as possible. "I thought you were very brave out there, Alice," she said.

"I didn't feel very brave," Alice replied. "I just wanted everyone to know the truth."

"And I'm glad you did. But I'm going to have to suspend your membership of the Grove. It wouldn't be fair to the others if I didn't."

Alice nodded. "I know," she said, "it's what I expected."

"But she's only here for a few more days, Tina," said Ben. "What's the point?"

"The point is, Ben, that I've got to be fair, and I've got to be seen to be fair. I can't have one rule for Alice and another rule for everyone else."

"Well, if Alice is suspended, then I'm not coming back either," said Ben petulantly. "I don't care about the Grove, anyway."

"Don't say that, Ben, please," said Alice. "You don't mean it and I don't want to cause you any more trouble. I've done enough."

"Just calm down, Ben," said Tina. "I'm going to suspend Alice for a couple of days initially, and then we can look at it again. I have to think of everyone here."

Ben was tempted to continue with the argument. But he stopped himself. He knew that Tina was being perfectly fair.

"I think you should leave now, Alice," she said. "We'll let things settle down for a couple of days and see what happens. Maybe you'll be able to come back before the end of the week."

As Ben and Alice left the Grove they could hear raised voices coming from the general room but, fortunately for Alice, they didn't linger in the corridor long enough to hear exactly what was being said.

A few minutes later, a delegation made up of Sita, Teraise and Nat arrived at Tina's office.

"What can I do for you?" said Tina, looking up from her paperwork.

"We've been talking," said Nat.

"I gathered that," Tina replied.

"We know it's your decision on what happens but we thought we had the right to tell you what we felt about it."

"Of course you do."

"So we had a vote."

"Did you?"

"On whether we think Alice should be allowed back at the Grove."

Tina sighed. "And?"

"It wasn't unanimous," said Sita. "It was close."

"Yeah, it was close," agreed Nat. "But there was a majority decision."

"And what did the majority decide?" asked Tina, knowing only too well the answer she was about to receive.

"Well," said Nat, "the majority of us are against her coming back to the Grove. Ever."

Tina sighed for a second time. "I see," she said. "Well, thank you for telling me."

• • • • •

Ben and Alice parted at the end of the drive. Alice said that Ben should stay now that he was reinstated, but Ben told her he had had enough of the Grove, and the Grovers, for one day. He was still angry with the way Alice's apology had been received by some of his friends.

"I'll come back to Emma's with you," he offered. "You'll have to tell Emma's mum now. I'll help you."

"No, Ben," Alice replied. "You've done enough for me. More than enough. This time I've got to do it for myself."

So they parted, promising each other they would meet again the following day.

Alice walked slowly back to Emma's house. It had been an emotional and traumatic day so far, but it wasn't over yet. She had to tell Emma and her aunt everything. And it wouldn't be easy. When Alice had left that morning she and Emma had hardly been speaking to each other, and Emma's mum had no idea what had been going on over the past couple of days.

Alice walked up to the house, stopped at the back door, took a deep breath and went inside. Emma and her mum were in the kitchen.

"Hello, Alice," said her aunt with a smile. "Had a good day?"

Alice didn't mean to smile and she certainly didn't mean to laugh. But after the awful day she had had, she couldn't help it. She smiled. And then she laughed.

"Well, it's good to see you smiling at least," said Emma's mum. "Isn't it Emma?"

"Suppose so," said Emma grumpily. Emma had spent a miserable day. After Regina's early morning visit she had spent the rest of the day alone, knowing that all her friends would be enjoying themselves at the Grove.

"There's something I want to tell you," said Alice. "Both of you."

"What's that, then, love?" said Emma's mum.

"I think you'd better sit down, Auntie Jackie."

Alice began her story. She left nothing out, and was as honest with her aunt as she had been with Lou earlier in the day. And just like Lou, Emma's mum listened without interrupting.

Her face was grave and concerned as she listened. She was dismayed to hear all that had happened to her niece during her week at the Grove, and when Alice reached the final part of the story, the events of that particular day, Emma's face grew equally grave and concerned.

"So I'm suspended from the Grove," said Alice as she completed her unhappy story. "I'm sorry, Auntie Jackie. For everything. And I'm sorry that you and Emma are the last people I've apologised to. You should have been the first."

"I'm just glad that you have told us, pet," said her aunt. She got up and went over to the kettle. "I need a cup of tea after that. I'm not sure what to say. I need to think."

She filled the kettle and switched it on. No-one knew what to say next so they sat and watched the kettle, listening to the water bubble and gurgle as it got hotter and hotter. The water boiled, the kettle switched itself off and a long cloud of steam came billowing out through the spout.

"That's you, Alice," said Emma's mum as she made her tea. "That steam. The pressure's been building up ever since your mum and dad split up. Something had to give."

Alice didn't answer.

"But why didn't you talk to me? Why didn't you tell me how bad you were feeling?"

Alice shook her head. "I don't know. I wanted to. I've been wanting to talk about it for ages."

Her aunt went to the fridge, took out a carton of milk and poured a little into a tea cup.

"Just like your father," she said. "He's never been able to talk about things that really matter. He was like that even when we were kids. And you're much more like him than I realised."

She poured her tea and sat at the table. "So you're banned from the Grove?"

"Tina said for a couple of days. And then she'd see what happened."

"Well, maybe it'll be alright, then. You'll just have to stay here with Emma for the next two days. You wouldn't mind that, would you, Emma?"

"No, I wouldn't mind," said Emma. "I did mind today. It was such a waste of time. But if it helps, and then Alice can come back…"

"No," said Alice, interrupting her cousin. "I was thinking about it when I was walking back. I'd like to go home. I'd like to see you again, soon, and I'd make sure we didn't have an awful time like we did this time. But I'd like to go home now. I want to see my mum."

"Do you love?" asked her aunt with a smile.

"I really do. Can I phone her tonight?"

"Why don't you let me phone her? I think you've done enough explaining for one day."

Alice nodded. "Thanks, Auntie Jackie," she said. "Would you ask her if she'll come and get me tomorrow?"

• • • • •

The two mums hadn't spoken to each other for a long time, not since Alice's parents had split up. Before then, they had been good friends, talking on the telephone regularly, and seeing each other quite often.

But Alice's dad and Emma's mum were brother and sister, and with the break-up of the marriage, the two friends had drifted apart.

It wasn't deliberate. Neither of the two women wanted the friendship with the other one to end. It was just difficult. Embarrassing. Awkward.

Emma's mum hadn't made contact partly because she felt she had to be loyal to her brother, even though she wouldn't take sides in any arguments.

Alice's mum hadn't made contact because she thought Emma's mum would think she had to be loyal to her brother, even though she wouldn't have asked her to take sides in any arguments.

And so, despite wanting to talk to each other, they hadn't.

But that night, after the girls had gone up to Emma's room, Emma's mum phoned Alice's mum.

"Hello?"

"Hello, Helen," said Emma's mum, slightly nervously. "It's Jackie."

"Jackie!" said Alice's mum. "Oh, it's so good to hear from you!"

After that, the two friends had a long conversation.

At the same time, their two daughters were also having a long conversation and, just like their mothers, they too were rebuilding their friendship.

Emma and Alice had spent a difficult week together, their friendship had been stretched almost to breaking point. But as they talked, without secrets to keep or feelings to hide, they grew closer again. Good friends. Just like they always had been.

They talked and talked, and then Alice said she had to write a letter. To Ben. She couldn't go back to the Grove but she wanted to say goodbye.

• • • • •

"I suppose you know?" said Regina.

"Know what?" Emma replied.

"Your cousin. She's suspended. She must have told you."

"Yes, she told us. She told us everything."

"Not everything," said Regina. "She doesn't know everything. We had a vote after she went, all of us, and we don't want her to come back."

"She won't be coming back, Regina," said Emma. "Her mum came to pick her up this morning."

"Oh," said Regina as she watched Emma walk away and go into the office. "Oh."

For the next few minutes, Emma sat in the office with Tina and described the events of the previous evening and that morning.

"Oh, well," said Tina. "Perhaps it's for the best."

"She asked me to say thanks to you, though," said Emma. "And she meant it, I know she did."

"I know she did, too," said Tina.

Emma wasn't looking forward to seeing Ben. But she had promised her cousin that she would deliver the letter into his hands. She waited anxiously and, eventually, Ben turned up. He didn't look happy.

"Where's Alice?" he said when he spotted Emma in the general room.

"She's..." Emma stopped and took an envelope from her coat pocket. "She asked me to give you this letter."

Ben looked confused.

"Why's she written to me? Where is she?"

"Just read the letter, Ben," said Emma.

Ben tore open the letter and began to read. The general room was crowded and everyone was looking in Ben's direction. Everyone knew by now that Alice had gone home. Everyone but Ben.

He stood and read the letter, completely unaware that the Grovers were watching him.

He read the first page, and then the second and then the third. And then he read the whole letter again. From start to finish.

He folded the letter, put it in his pocket, and looked at Emma. "But she promised," he said.

Emma didn't answer. There was nothing she could say.

Ben sighed. He turned away and walked out, and he wasn't seen at the Grove again that day.

• • • • •

"Can I speak to Alice, please?"

"Who is it?"

"It's Ben."

"Oh, Ben, I've heard a lot about you."

"Oh."

"Don't worry, they were all good things. Just hang on, I'll get her for you."

Ben waited, and a few moments later Alice picked up the telephone receiver.

"Ben!"

"Hello, Alice."

"I've missed you."

"I've missed you too."

"So, how was it?"

"What?"

"You know what. The party."

"It was alright. You should have been there."

"Ben, you know I couldn't. I had to come home. Come on, tell me about it."

"What d'you want to know?"

"Everything."

"Well… there was a bonfire, and they'd put candles in the trees, and on the tables."

"It sounds lovely. Romantic."

"Well, it could have been, if you'd been there."

"Go on, what else?"

"We had a barbecue. Ollie and Liam did the cooking."

"Did they?"

"It was alright. No-one got food poisoning. Miracle. Then there was entertainment, if you could call it that. Remember that little kid, Bradley?"

"Of course I do. He won the poster competition."

"Yeah, well, he's a magician as well. He did some tricks. You could see how he was doing them. It was easy. Then Sita and Karen and Cher did some singing."

"Was it good?"

"Yeah, it was. There was dancing."

"What sort of dancing?"

"You know, sort of slow dancing."

"Did everyone dance?"

"A lot of them."

"Did you dance?"

"I… I wasn't going to. But Tina said I should."

"Who did you dance with?"

"Claire."

"That blond girl?"

"Yeah."

"She's nice-looking."

"She's alright."

"Do you like her?"

"I like you."

"How many dances did you have with her?"

"I dunno. A couple."

"Oh."

"I wouldn't have danced with her if you'd been there. And you could have been, I know you could. A lot of them have changed their minds. They were saying that you shouldn't have been suspended. Or that you should have been allowed to come back for the party."

"I had to come home, Ben."

"Yeah… I suppose so. What's been happening, since you got back?"

"Mum's been brilliant. We've had a really good talk. And I'm seeing my dad tomorrow. Mum and him have had a talk as well. I think things might start to get better now."

"Good. I'm glad. We took the posters round the town today. They're in loads of shops. I could send you one, if you want."

"I don't think so, Ben. I think I've seen enough of that poster."

"Yeah. I'd better go, Alice."

"Oh."

"I don't want to. Lou doesn't like us being on the phone for too long."

"Alright. Say hello to Lou for me."

"I will."

"Ben?"

"Yeah?"

"Are you going out with Claire?"

"No."

"Oh. Good. You will phone me again, then?"

"Yeah. 'Course. Or you could phone me."

"I will. Bye, then, Ben."

"Bye, Alice."

"Put the phone down, then."

"You put it down first."

"No, you."

"No, you."
"We'll put it down at the same time."
"Alright, then."
"After three."
"Yeah."
"Ready?"
"Yeah."
"Bye, Ben."
"Bye, Alice."
"One... two... three."
They put down the telephone receivers at exactly the same moment.

THE END

If you enjoyed this book, why not read about Stumpy and Wombat in

No laughing matter

also by Robert Rigby

For information on Two-Can books and multimedia, call (0)20 7224 2440, fax (0)20 7224 7005, or visit our website at http://www.two-canpublishing.com

LONDON • PRINCETON